P9-DDW-920

## *Screw rational.*

Adelaide was a grown woman with agency over her body and actions.

"That's fine as long as you let your grandmother know your whereabouts. She was very worried about you."

"Stop treating me like a child, Michael." Adelaide tugged down his tie so he would look her in the eye. "This is the last time I give you a warning. If you ever patronize me again, I will punch you in the throat *without* hesitation."

Her vicious snarl did nothing to diminish her beauty, and something feral flared low in his gut.

They stood frozen, as their anger and frustration burned hotter, until something volatile and fierce permeated the space between them.

Michael's hand wrapped around the back of her neck as Adelaide gasped, tilting her head back in silent invitation.

Michael was hot, hungry and dizzy.

He was nothing but this moment... Nothing but need.

\* \* \*

*Secret Crush Seduction* by Jayci Lee is part of The Heirs of Hansol series.

Dear Reader,

Thank you for continuing on this journey with me by choosing *Secret Crush Seduction*, book two in The Heirs of Hansol series. I hope you enjoy reading Adelaide and Michael's story and their well-deserved happily-ever-after as much as I enjoyed writing it.

Writing this book meant a great deal to me because it helped me believe in myself as a writer. It reminded me that I could sit down and write a book from start to finish. That being a published author was part of my life now. It feels incredible and it wouldn't be possible without you—my reader.

As I write this letter to you, I have already completed book three, featuring Colin Song and Jihae Park as the main characters. I'm so excited for you to meet them. But one book at a time.

Happy readings!

Love,

*Jayci*

# JAYCI LEE

——

## SECRET CRUSH SEDUCTION

If you purchased this book without a cover you should be aware that this book is stolen property. It was reported as "unsold and destroyed" to the publisher, and neither the author nor the publisher has received any payment for this "stripped book."

**HARLEQUIN®**

# DESIRE™

Recycling programs
for this product may
not exist in your area.

ISBN-13: 978-1-335-20935-1

Secret Crush Seduction

Copyright © 2020 by Judith J. Yi

All rights reserved. No part of this book may be used or reproduced in any manner whatsoever without written permission except in the case of brief quotations embodied in critical articles and reviews.

This is a work of fiction. Names, characters, places and incidents are either the product of the author's imagination or are used fictitiously. Any resemblance to actual persons, living or dead, businesses, companies, events or locales is entirely coincidental.

This edition published by arrangement with Harlequin Books S.A.

For questions and comments about the quality of this book, please contact us at CustomerService@Harlequin.com.

Harlequin Enterprises ULC
22 Adelaide St. West, 40th Floor
Toronto, Ontario M5H 4E3, Canada
www.Harlequin.com

**Printed in U.S.A.**

**Jayci Lee** writes poignant, sexy and laugh-out-loud romance every free second she can scavenge. She lives in sunny California with her tall, dark and handsome husband, two amazing boys with boundless energy, and a fluffy rescue whose cuteness is a major distraction. At times, she cannot accommodate reality because her brain is full of drool-worthy heroes and badass heroines clamoring to come to life.

Because of all the books demanding to be written, Jayci writes full-time now and is semiretired from her fifteen-year career as a defense litigator. She loves food, wine and traveling, and, incidentally, so do her characters. Books have always helped her grow, dream and heal, and she hopes her books will do the same for you.

### Books by Jayci Lee

### Harlequin Desire

### *The Heirs of Hansol*

*Temporary Wife Temptation*
*Secret Crush Seduction*

Visit her Author Profile page at Harlequin.com, or jaycilee.com, for more titles.

You can also find Jayci Lee on Facebook, along with other Harlequin Desire authors, at Facebook.com/harlequindesireauthors!

To Mom, thank you for passing on the stubborn tenacity and teaching me the good work ethic to keep on writing my beloved books. I love you.

# One

*What the hell kind of boy band medley is this?*

A handful of young women—much younger than Adelaide Song's twenty-six years—were spinning around in a circle on the dance floor at Pendulum, screaming along to some bubblegum pop song. It was early in the evening, and they were sloppy drunk.

Adelaide was most definitely *not* in the mood to play Ring Around the Rosie at her cousin Colin's nightclub. After the face-off she'd just had with her grandmother, she needed to lose herself in good music and dance off her frustration.

What was the Tuesday DJ doing up there on a Friday night anyway? She hunted down Tucker, the top DJ and manager-in-training, to remedy the situation.

"Hi, Tucker."

"Hey, Adelaide. You haven't been in for a while. How are you doing?"

"I've had better days." She smiled wryly. "Why is Ethan up there? I can really do without the over-the-top pop tonight. It's a Saturday night. Let's get some real jam going." Adelaide looked over her shoulder and out into the club. "By the way, where's Colin?"

"He had a meeting and asked me to hold down the fort." The heavily pierced and tattooed DJ stared at his shoes and fidgeted under her scrutiny. "Ethan begged me to let him play for an hour, and I felt bad for the guy. He's a good kid."

"A good kid who is playing Tuesday night pop on a Saturday night."

"I got you. I'll take over," he said with a shy smile.

"Thank you. You're the best."

And it was true. He was an immensely talented DJ, and he should be proud of his mad skills. Within minutes, the sensuous, liberating strains of Tucker's magic filled the air and calmed the tremors of frustration quaking under Adelaide's skin.

For the last two years since she'd finished her MBA, Adelaide had been begging her grandmother to let her take her place at Hansol Corporation—the family's multibillion-dollar apparel empire—but her answer was always, "Maybe next year." It broke Adelaide's heart because those words really meant that Grandmother still hadn't forgiven her for her wild years in college.

It had been a time of switching from boyfriend to boyfriend, partying too hard to care about classes and distancing herself from the family. It wasn't until her last year in college that she'd rediscovered her thirst for knowledge. She had cleaned up her act and learned to balance her responsibilities and recreations. That was nearly six years ago. But to her family, she was still an irresponsible wild child incapable of contributing anything of worth to Hansol. She felt a twinge of shame at her desperate plea to her grandmother. *I'm not that kid anymore.*

Refusing to let herself drown in sadness, Adelaide strode to the dance floor with sharp clicks of her stilettos and headed for a corner stage raised three feet from the floor. She gripped the railing when she reached the top and exhaled through pursed lips. Then she closed her eyes and let the music flow through her. The rhythm always grew in the pit of her gut and spread to her hips, legs, then the rest of her body. When it filled her to the brim, she danced.

Everything disappeared as it always did. Her loneliness. Her insecurities. Her grandmother with her dismissive words and disappointed eyes. They all shrank and blurred as she moved her body, carried away by the music and its beat.

Her song came on. The bass in the music shook the dance floor and pounded in her blood. Primal and raw. She closed her eyes and lifted her arms above her head, tracing the outlines of the song with her body. She no longer existed. There was the song and she was its instrument. Adelaide wasn't there anymore. She just danced. Danced until she was erased.

She heard a rough growl from beside her. The sound merged with the music in its feral possessiveness. It wasn't until a pair of strong hands grasped her upper arms that she realized a person had emitted the sound. A very tall, blazingly furious man person.

"Goddammit, Addy. What are you doing here?"

"Good to see you, too," she said with cool detachment.

Inside, she shivered with awareness and need that refused to be stilled. *Michael* Reynolds. Her older brother's best friend, and her first love. Unrequited, of course. He treated her like she was his kid sister for the most part. In the meantime, she was burning up from his innocuous touch.

"Let me take you home," he said. "Your grandmother's worried about you."

*Damn it.* She wasn't finished flushing out the anger and melancholy from her system. Her insecurities were rampaging in her mind, and she couldn't handle any more heartache tonight. So she closed her eyes again and danced to make Michael disappear, as well.

Since he still held her arms, she placed her hands on his broad chest and assumed the junior high slow dance position. But rather than shift awkwardly from foot to foot, she swerved her body in languid waves in time with the music. Michael stood frozen for a few beats, then expelled a sound between a cough and curse.

"I'm taking you home. Now." He abruptly picked her up off the floor with an arm under her thighs and the other cradling her back, frowning down at her with the same look everyone bestowed on her. Disappointment.

*Enough.*

"Stop with the Kevin Costner impersonation, and put me down," she said, pushing against his shoulder.

"No way." A hint of humor sparked in his eyes. "I

remember how fast you can run. I'm not in the mood to chase you."

Adelaide spied movement from the corner of her eyes. The club bouncers were heading toward them with fists clenched. They knew she was Colin's cousin and were a protective lot, and Michael was carrying her out of the club, looking angry as hell.

"Oh, for God's sake. I'm not a ten-year-old, Michael." She struggled in earnest. If the idiot didn't put her down, he would get beaten to a pulp by the bouncers before she could de-escalate the situation. "You need to put me down. I'll walk out with you."

"Adelaide? You all right?" *Too late.* Four of the loyal bouncers had surrounded them. "I suggest you get your hands off of her, buddy."

"I suggest you go back to your posts, gentlemen." Michael's arms tightened around her, and a dark, reck-lessness entered his eyes. Why was he acting like this? "I'm escorting *Ms. Song* home."

A baseball mitt–sized hand with an impressively large signet ring closed around Michael's shoulder. He tensed for a second then he loosened his arms and set her down. *Now he's letting me go? I'm the only thing between the giant fist and his face.*

Adelaide spun around to face the guys and plastered the back of her body against Michael's chest and thighs. Reaching her arms behind her, she held tight to what-ever part of him she could reach. She wouldn't be able to hold on to him if he really wanted to move, but she could hopefully slow him down. Every second was pre-cious for de-escalating the impending disaster.

When his body went taut and hard, Adelaide flexed

her hands, wondering if he was getting ready to pounce. Through the roar of her instinct to protect him, she belatedly realized which part of his body she was holding—the exact point where his incredible ass met the back of his thighs. She gingerly cupped her hands to make certain.

*Yup. I'm grabbing his ass.*

She released his backside faster than she could gasp and gripped the sides of his pants in her fists, gathering as much fabric into her hands as possible.

"Settle down, guys." She injected her voice with steel to hide the slight tremor behind it. "My big brother decided to send his best friend to rescue me from myself. You know…from the drinking, dancing and general debauchery."

To her gratification, all the bouncers sputtered in outrage at the very idea. At least they knew what she was made of. She could take care of herself and then some.

"I know, I know. It's ridiculous, but he's practically my brother. Sometimes he treats me like the little girl I was when we were growing up together. He must see some invisible pigtails on my head." She scanned the immediate vicinity and saw the beginnings of curious eyes swiveling their way. "But you guys are my friends and know I can handle this, right? So please go back to work before we create a bigger scene."

As the mountainous bouncers retreated, baring their teeth at Michael for good measure, Adelaide stepped away from him. He felt the loss of her warmth acutely. Michael wanted to draw her back to him and return her small, strong hands to his ass. *Hell*. He was a complete dick. This was Adelaide. Garrett's baby sister.

She was right. He practically was her brother. He'd watched her grow from an adorable baby with alarmingly pudgy cheeks to an angry, sullen teenager. In many ways, he'd continued to think of her as that rebellious teen rather than the grown woman she was now. *But practically her brother?* Her words settled like a lump of coal in his stomach.

"Come," Adelaide commanded between gritted teeth, grabbing his hand in a death grip, and led them toward the exit.

He followed without argument.

When Mrs. Song called to ask him to check on Adelaide, Michael had tensed with concern. Grace Song was not a woman who fussed. She ruled Hansol Corporation and her extended family with an iron rod and swung it with chilling accuracy as needed.

If the formidable Song family matriarch had a soft spot, it would be for her only granddaughter. In her eyes, Addy was still the seven-year-old girl who'd lost her mom to cancer, which had caused her father to withdraw into his grief. Both parents, suddenly out of reach. Mrs. Song granted Adelaide more leeway than any of her children or grandchildren. If she was reeling her granddaughter in, something big must've happened.

Michael had shoved aside a pile of work to come searching for Adelaide, and found her dancing on a stage at Colin's club with hungry eyes ogling her. Fury swelled in his throat just thinking about it. Michael gripped Adelaide's hand more firmly and steered her toward his car. It had taken everything he had not to shove away the men surrounding her. He had no right or reason to feel possessive of her, but in that moment, his mind had screamed that she was his. Which he chalked up to temporary insanity.

"What the hell is going on, Addy?" He pulled her close to his car and placed his hands on her shoulders. "You were making a spectacle of yourself."

Adelaide winced and jerked out of his hold. He'd hurt her with his hard, judgmental words, and he immediately regretted them. But he'd wanted to lash out at her. The memory of her dancing on the stage like a siren and the men gathered around her had triggered something inside him. The dismay, fury and…lust that swirled inside him in that moment unhinged him. He was confused and angry with himself, and a little angry with her even though she'd done nothing to deserve it. He felt like he was falling headfirst into an abyss, but that was his problem. It wasn't fair to drag her down with him.

"What are you doing here?" she asked, her expression schooled into a bored, sardonic smirk.

Michael ran his hand through his hair and tugged a fistful at the top of his head. His scalp felt stretched too tight.

"So her majesty, Grace Song, summoned you to check on me." Angry splashes of color stained her cheeks. "Since when have you been her errand boy?"

"Addy…"

"Don't. Call. Me. That." She pivoted and marched away from him.

"Damn it." He went after her and stopped her trajectory by taking a firm grip of her hand. "She's worried about you. Worried enough to call me to find you. What happened between you two?"

"We argued because I'm sick of being treated like a child. Ironically, I ran out of the house sobbing like one." The rage vibrating through Adelaide seeped out of her, and her shoulders drooped in fatigue. "I could understand why she's worried. She hasn't seen me cry since I was seven. But enough is enough. I can't go on like this."

Now he understood why Mrs. Song had called him. Adelaide's older brother, Garrett, was in New York with his wife and daughter, and Colin was probably unreachable. She had wanted this kept close to the family. Michael wasn't family, but growing up, he'd spent more time at the Songs' than at home. Plus, he was their publicist. She knew he'd be discreet about whatever state he found Adelaide in.

"I'm ready take my place at Hansol, but *Hal-muh-nee* shut me down with another 'maybe next year.' Hansol is my family's legacy, and I want to be a part of its future." Adelaide's voice trailed off into a sad, forlorn sigh, and Michael wrapped his arms around her. He wanted to chase her sadness away, but the best he could do was listen. "She's been saying that for the last two years. And next time when I ask her again, it'll be the same answer. She doesn't believe I have anything to contribute. I'm nothing but a clueless child to her."

"That can't be true. You're one of the smartest people I know," he said, running his hand through the silky strands of her long hair. Her arms tightened around him. "You're far from being a clueless child, and your grandmother knows that better than anyone."

"Then why is she keeping me out of Hansol?" She leaned back to meet his eyes. "She's afraid I'll tarnish Hansol's reputation. She hasn't forgiven me for my college days. Most of the crap in the tabloids didn't even have a grain of truth in them. Yes, I partied hard and dated more than my fair share of guys, but I'm not an eighteen-year-old anymore."

"I can't imagine your grandmother being that small-minded. There has to be another reason, but you know her better than me. Besides, if that's what you think, there's an easy fix." His arms still encircled her waist, and he was drawing slow circles on her lower back. When his brain registered what his hand was doing, he coughed and dropped his arms.

Adelaide arched an eyebrow and crossed her arms. He didn't know if it was because she was waiting to hear his suggestion or because of his hurried step away from her. "Tell me more about this easy fix."

His mind went blank. Her crossed arms had the effect of a bustier, pulling her breasts close and lifting them high. The sexy-as-hell scene at the club must have short-circuited his brain. He beat away his heightened awareness and focused on the shadowy outlines of the plan that had formed in his head.

"You majored in fashion design, right?"

"Along with sociology. And I have an MBA."

"Even better." Michael rubbed his hands together. "Hansol's Corporate Social Responsibility Department has funds to support various charities. I think you should pitch a big-scale charity event, and show your grandmother and the world that you have what it takes to plan and execute it."

"You're right. There are a million things I could do." Her face lit up with excitement. "Where do I start?"

"With the CSR Department. They're the ones you need to convince to sign off on your proposal."

A slow smile curved her lips, then she launched herself at him with a giddy laugh. His heart sang with her happiness, and he lifted her off her feet and hugged her tight. Dizzy and breathless from her nearness, Michael forced himself to set her down. Before he could gather his scattered wits, Adelaide reached up and placed a lingering kiss on his cheek.

"Thank you, Michael." Her wide eyes were bright and welcoming, and he had to muster every last ounce of willpower not to kiss her upturned face. He needed to nip whatever this was in the bud.

"Sure thing, kiddo." He slid the back of his index finger down her perfect nose—something he'd done since she was a little girl.

Adelaide jerked back and shoved his hand away, her eyes burning with resentment. Regret washed over him. She hated being treated like a child, and he hated himself for using her vulnerability to push her away. He was desperate, but he should've found a better way to distance himself.

As expected, Adelaide pivoted on her heels and walked off without a word. Even the back of her head looked furious with him.

# Two

Adelaide's annoyance with Michael cooled off as she drove home, her thoughts meandering down way-back-when lane. She'd fallen in love with Michael Reynolds when she still pronounced her *r*'s as *w*'s. He was her brother Garrett's best friend and she'd worshipped the two of them. After an especially spectacular day of playing pirates, she'd asked her big brother to marry her. He'd gently reminded her they couldn't get married since they were brother and sister. Naturally, she had to marry Michael, instead. At the tender age of four, she'd been too shy to ask him, but she'd vowed to propose to him when she grew up.

It was a good thing she got over her infatuation with him. Otherwise, she would've grown ancient waiting for him to realize she was a grown woman when he could think of her only as a "kiddo." Besides, he had broken her heart when he married someone else during her senior year in high school.

Adelaide used to be a bigmouthed teenager with zero dating experience, but from all her talk and posturing, her friends thought she was a sex guru. At age seventeen, she hadn't even kissed a boy. She'd guarded all her firsts for Michael because she already belonged to him. Or so her silly mind had thought. With him away in la-la land with his wife, Adelaide had made up for lost time. By the end of her senior year, she'd efficiently checked off all the firsts on her list.

After his divorce, Michael reclaimed his role as the Song family's only blond member, but things hadn't been the same between them. He maintained his stupid, goofy demeanor, but a light seemed to have gone out of him. When she came home from college, she tried to talk to him and draw him out. But all that got her was a wall of indifference and ever-growing distance.

She understood what she'd felt for him was a childhood crush. A long-term infatuation. The past didn't matter anymore. All she wanted was her friend and confidant back, but Michael had shut her out so completely they were no better than casual acquaintances. The loss of their friendship hurt more than watching him marry someone who wasn't her.

Adelaide growled in frustration and leaned hard on the gas, passing a car with less than a foot to spare. The blaring horn brought some sense back into her. The moral of the day was to prove to the world that she *wasn't* juvenile. She was off to a bleak start.

If she wanted to be taken seriously, she had to prove

to her grandmother that she was born to lead Hansol just like her brother. Garrett was the business mastermind, but Adelaide had the creativity Hansol needed to reach the next level through innovative apparel.

Michael had made a good point before frustrating her out of her mind with the *kiddo* bullcrap. With her background in fashion design and sociology, and a mint-condition MBA, she could produce a charity event that would have the guests rushing the stage crying, *Please, take my money!*

Adelaide stopped at a red light and drummed her fingers on the steering wheel. This was ridiculous. *Why do I have to prove myself?* They practically dragged Garrett into the company as soon as he finished his MBA degree. She'd finished hers two years ago with better grades than her brother, but no one had come begging for her presence at Hansol. She puffed up her cheeks and blew out a long breath.

Perhaps it had something to do with the fact that her big brother had interned at Hansol and learned the ropes every summer since his freshman year in college. She, on the other hand, had partied like it was 1969 and barely passed her classes. But how could they punish her for her reckless youth for all these years? It was completely unfair, but that was life. She would prove herself to the world and get on with her dreams.

*What am I good at?* No, that wasn't the right question to ask first. *What do I care most about?*

Her college roommate and best friend, Kate immediately came to mind.

Kate had a younger brother on the autism spectrum. Adelaide spent a lot of time with Kate and her family, who lived locally, and became good friends with her younger brother. Stu was an amazing person with too many incredible talents to count and a wicked sense of humor. But being a person with autism, he had a penchant for social faux-pas.

Stu was teased and bullied at school much too often. The saddest part was he didn't understand when his classmates were being cruel to him. One time his so-called best friend, Ken, told him he didn't want to hang out with him anymore. Stu assumed he meant just for that particular day, so he continued seeking his friend out every day. Even when he got the cold shoulder again and again, Stu made excuses for Ken, saying he must've been tired or he must've had a bad day. And he always found his best friend, and talked to him as if the day before hadn't happened. Eventually Ken made it crystal clear to Stu that he meant forever. *You are not my friend anymore. I can't stand seeing your stupid face every day. Stay away from me!*

Stu had told Kate and Adelaide about what happened in his most casual voice. Without anger or sorrow. He didn't understand his heart was broken. But slowly he withdrew into himself, confused and scared. It took him months to find his peace. Months of no art or music. Months of no laughter.

If only they could've kept him away from the unkind world. Locked him away in a cocoon of love and support, where the outside couldn't intrude. But that would have been unfair to Stu and the world, because he was meant to do great things with his life. He was meant to make the world a better place. Adelaide never doubted that. He was that amazing.

It tore at Adelaide's heart to know that people with autism were misunderstood and made fun of for their quirks and challenges. Most people laughing and yelling at them didn't even realize they had autism. Even if they knew, they didn't understand what autism spectrum disorder really was.

Maybe she could use her charity event to raise autism awareness. Her pulse doubled in speed as excitement coursed through her. Adelaide Song was ready to change the world. The next question was *how?*

What were her strengths? Fashion. People. Finance. And thanks to her wild days, she knew what a good party should look like. An idea began forming in her head, glimmering like a mirage. She thought back to how she'd taken a course in college on designing clothing for people with special needs. What if she staged an exclusive fashion show featuring fashion-forward, sensory-friendly clothing—from tagless, flat-seamed suits and cocktail dresses to formal wear that people with autism could be comfortable in? There was no reason Stu and others like him shouldn't be able to dress with amazing creative flair. They should also have formal wear for special events. They deserved options beyond black sweatpants and black tennis shoes.

Adelaide bounced in her seat, too pumped up to stay still.

She wanted to design some of the clothes, but she would also have an open contest at local colleges where students could submit their ideas. Maybe the winner could get a summer internship at Hansol.

Adelaide couldn't hold back her squeal. *Oh, my God.* She could do this.

She turned into the driveway of the Songs' Pacific Palisades home, and parked her car near the front door. Liliana, their housekeeper, was going to give her a tongue-lashing tomorrow for blocking the road, but Adelaide was low on battery without a charger to plug herself into. When she dragged herself to her room, she brushed her teeth and splashed some water on her face. No seven-step Korean skin care for her tonight. She snuggled under her soft comforter and buried her face against her puffy cloud of a pillow.

Adelaide wanted to ride her elation and dream sparkly dreams, but the ambitious, practical side of her brain refused to shut up. The big picture was there, but it would be useless without the proper execution. She had to create the hype, connect with the big-name donors. She needed someone with a solid reputation and the right connections to help execute the event.

Her palms grew damp with sweat and she gnawed on her bottom lip, suddenly wide-awake. She knew the perfect person for the job. The problem was he'd never agree to work with her. Despite what he'd said to her, he was no different from her family and treated her like an overgrown child.

Besides, he didn't want to be near her if at all possible. When they spent time together at family gatherings or social functions, he barely acknowledged her. More often than not, he went out of his way to avoid her altogether. No matter what nice brotherly things he'd said earlier tonight, he still thought of her as a lost cause.

A flash of hurt cut a bright red line across her heart. What was so wrong with her? She bit down hard on her lip and tasted blood, hoping the pain would shock her insecurities out of her. The emotional lashings she'd received that day rolled through her, and hot tears stung her eyes.

Michael wouldn't want to be personally involved in her project. But that only meant Adelaide shouldn't give him a chance to refuse. He was going to help her pull off this event, and she would convince him, her grandmother and the world that she wasn't a spoiled, good-for-nothing heiress once and for all.

Hey, Michael.

It was a text from Adelaide. This was the first time he'd heard from her since she'd walked away from him at the nightclub parking lot. His heart vibrated like a gong that had been rung with too much enthusiasm. Which was ridiculous. He was ridiculous. He'd just been worried about her. That's all.

Hey. He cringed at his lame reply and stared intently at the skipping ellipses on his screen.

Grandmother wants to invite you to dinner.

"Invite" me?

LOL. Don't be silly. I was just being diplomatic. You've been summoned to the Song residence for dinner.

He grinned broadly. Failure to comply would result in terrifying consequences. He had no clue as to what Machiavellian punishments Grace Song would bestow, but the fear of not knowing was probably worse.

I wouldn't miss it for the world.

You're such a chicken. ^__^

No, I'm a smart man with finely tuned survival instincts.

He shook with quiet laughter. Villainizing Mrs. Song used to be his and Garrett's favorite game. They'd come up with one ludicrous scenario after another that would lead to Mrs. Song's horrifying punishments. Adelaide had never liked that game. She would eventually burst into tears because they were making fun of her grandma. For him and Garrett, it was a way to cope with the woman's larger-than-life persona—like drawing a mustache on a dictator's portrait. Adelaide, who saw everyone in their best light, didn't understand why they were intimidated by her *hal-muh-nee.*

Whatever. We'll see you at 19:00 sharp. Pro Tip: She's been into macarons lately.

Not the matcha jelly roll cake?

She's so over that.

Thanks for the heads-up. I'll stop by Bottega Louie on my way over.

Michael's unease with the Song family matriarch had melted away with time and maturity. She now had his unadulterated respect and gratitude. He respected her for her work ethic, her vision and her sacrifices. He was grateful to her for being there for him when he had no one else. His parents went through a nasty divorce when he was eleven, and he couldn't bear to be home with them. Mrs. Song had accepted him into her home and her quiet support had meant more to him than anyone else's stilted reassurances.

When he found himself lost again, he'd gone to her because he trusted her implicitly. She was the only person who knew the real reason his marriage had fallen apart. As always, she'd been pragmatic and inspiring. She understood loss and pain. She knew what it took to survive. He'd never felt whole since then but knew he was worth something, thanks to her. He could still contribute to the world and make a difference, even if a wife and children were only pipe dreams to him.

Michael wrapped up work early so he could pick up the macarons. Fifteen minutes later, he left the bakery and walked to his car with a smile on his face and a precariously high macaron tower in his arms. He managed not to topple the thing and placed it carefully on the passenger seat floor. After slowly backing out of his parking spot, he drove toward Pacific Palisades never going past the speed limit. Although his body urged him to drive faster, he couldn't risk tipping over the tower, which he felt a little foolish for buying now that it sat swaying on the floor of his car.

When he finally pulled into the Songs' driveway, he parked off to the side in his usual spot. Juggling the vibrant pink, cream and sage tower in his arms, he rang the front door with his elbow.

The door to the Song residence opened before the

echoes of the doorbell died out. "Michael, it's been so long."

"Hello, Liliana." He leaned into the older woman's hug, holding the ridiculous macaron concoction to the side. "It's only been a couple months."

The Song household wouldn't be complete without their housekeeper, Liliana. Warm, sweet and omniscient, she knew the Songs inside and out, and cared for them with fierce loyalty. At the moment, she was eyeing the macaron tower with both brows raised high.

"It's… Like you said, it's been a while, so I thought I should bring something nice. For Mrs. Song. And Mr. Song. And you, too, of course."

"Miss Adelaide likes macarons, too, you know," she said with a wide grin.

"Yes. Of course, I know. She… It's for her, too. It's for all of you." *Goddammit.* He was tripping all over himself, and he didn't know what the hell Liliana was getting at. Irritated with himself, he handed over the macarons. "Please hold it for a second while I take my shoes off."

"Before you ask, I don't know why they've invited you over so suddenly," she whispered, taking the tower from him. "All I know is that Adelaide is a nervous wreck."

Michael's eyebrows rose into his hairline. "Adelaide?"

"Like I said, I don't know. But it's something big." When he straightened and took the tower off her hands, she leaned close and said, "Adelaide made dinner."

Adelaide cooked two days a year, and two days only. Thanksgiving and New Year's. She was a fantastic cook, and everyone looked forward to those two magical days, but she didn't step inside the kitchen at any other time.

She was definitely up to something, and he might be one of her targets. Once she softened everyone up with dinner, she would make her move and shock the hell out of them. It made no difference, though. Michael was not going to turn down a dinner prepared by Adelaide.

"She's in the kitchen."

"I know the way." With a grin, he strode down the hallway with sure-footed steps. He skidded to a stop at the kitchen entrance, nearly dropping his offering.

*Blooding hell.*

Adelaide had her back turned. She was in her cooking outfit. It wasn't anything special, really. A tight black shirt and tighter black jeans with a pure white apron wrapped around her waist. But it was the outfit that had first made Michael realize she wasn't a kid anymore.

It was about a year after his divorce, and she'd recently come home from college. They hadn't seen each other in years, and the sight of Adelaide all grown up had stolen his breath. She barely topped five feet, but every inch of her was toned and supple, with gentle curves in all the right places. He'd lost count of all the tempting spots that would fit perfectly into his hands. That was years ago, but the memory of Adelaide in that moment superimposed on the Adelaide standing in front of him left him weak in the knees.

He was a thirty-four-year-old divorced man with a train of baggage. He had no business ogling a woman nearly a decade younger than him. Especially since the woman was Garrett's little sister. Michael tore his gaze from her and swallowed after three attempts.

He stepped into the kitchen and quietly placed the macaron tower on the corner of the counter so it wouldn't interfere with Adelaide's cooking. Something smelled delicious and his mouth watered with anticipation. If his nose wasn't lying to him, she was making Korean food.

"Michael," she greeted him with a smile. "When did you get here?"

"Just now." He coughed into his fist, hoping she wouldn't notice the gift he had left on the counter. "Do you need any help?"

"Could you set the table for four and start setting out the *banchan*? One set on each side?" Adelaide scanned the kitchen with her chin in her hand, probably considering what else had to be done. He saw the exact moment she registered the colorful macaron tower. Her jaws went slack, then she blinked several times before bursting into laughter. "Are you trying to earn brownie points with my grandmother? That is so ridiculous for a dinner for four, but utterly irresistible because…macarons."

"You're welcome," he said, grinning, relieved Adelaide glossed over his lapse in judgment. "So your dad is having dinner with us?"

"Yup. The Songs are miraculously all home for dinner."

The thought of a family dinner, even with someone else's family, broadened his grin. Michael reached the utensils drawer in two steps, and picked out the silver spoon and chopsticks for the elders, and the generic silverware for him and Adelaide.

"So…" It was obvious she was orchestrating the lovely dinner with an ulterior motive. If he was lucky, she might let slip a hint of what she gunning for. "Do you know why Mrs. Song summoned me tonight?"

Adelaide shrugged noncommittally. "Maybe she wants to thank you for 'coming to my rescue' the other night."

"The way I remember it, I didn't exactly bring you safely home. You walked away from me and drove off into the night." He drew his brows together, realizing she could've driven to another nightclub to dance in a new crowd of men. "Where *did* you go that night?"

"None of your business." Her gaze turned glacial.

"It *is* my business," he said. She was 100 percent right about it being none of his business, but he suddenly felt very contrary. "I'm practically your big brother. Remember, sis?"

"Well, *oppa*." Angry sparks jumped in her eyes. "I got a few of my boy toys together for an all-night orgy. I hope that's okay with you."

"That's fine as long as you let your grandmother know your whereabouts." He ran his hands down his face. "Like I said, she was very worried about you."

"Stop treating me like a child, Michael." Adelaide stomped up to him and tugged down his tie so he would look her in the eye. "This is your last warning. If you ever patronize me again, I will punch you in the throat *without* hesitation."

Her vicious snarl did nothing to diminish her beauty, and something feral flared low in his gut. Their noses were nearly touching and they breathed each other in. They stood frozen, as their anger and frustration burned hotter, until something volatile and fierce permeated the empty space between them.

Without conscious thought on his part, Michael's hand rose and wrapped around the back of her neck. She gasped and tilted her head back in silent invitation, exposing the delicate triangle under her throat. Unable to resist, he leaned forward and brushed the tip of his nose on the sensitive skin behind her ear and traced his way down to where her neck met the curve of her shoulder. The space between them disappeared. Adelaide's hands were pressed flat on his back, and he pulled her closer. He was hot, hungry and dizzy. He was nothing but this moment… Nothing but need.

Michael inhaled her intoxicating scent—jasmine and verbena—and sighed in wonder. Something held him back from kissing her, and the effort was exhausting him. He slowly traced his way back up and pressed his cheek against hers. A small sigh escaped her and he smiled, journeying to her opposite cheek. This time he let his lips brush across her cheek and slide down her jaws. He needed to taste her. He was losing the will to fight. But fight what? He placed a lingering kiss on her neck with parted lips and blew softly on the damp spot, drawing a shiver from her. *Adelaide*.

With a jolt of alarm and a rush of air, he and Adelaide were suddenly standing at opposite ends of the kitchen table before his mind grasped what had happened. After several steadying breaths, he heard quiet, slippered footsteps coming down the hallway.

"Michael. Thank you for coming." Mrs. Song stood

in front of him with her hand extended. Her voice sounded faraway and muted, as though he was submerged under water. Somehow, he managed to fit his hand around hers, which she pulled back after a gentle squeeze. He noticed Adelaide's father standing next to her.

"Mrs. Song," he said, bending lightly at the waist in a proper greeting to both elders. "Mr. Song. It's great to see you."

"*James*. For heaven's sake, Mike. I've been asking you to call me James for over a decade." Adelaide's father smiled widely and slapped him on the back. "I miss my son's stoic mug. The least you could do is visit more often. Plus, you're the polar opposite of Garrett, so I'd enjoy your company more."

"Anytime, James." Michael laughed, unaccountably pleased. Not that he'd ever admit it, but he missed his best friend, too.

"That was a lovely reunion." Adelaide's tart comment brought him to a full stop.

He searched her face, but her cheeky, playful facade hid her true thoughts from him. It was a Song family superpower. They could don any mask in a split second and hide all their feelings behind it. It was annoying as hell on a good day, but he hated those masks with a vengeance now.

Backing away from his turbulent thoughts, Michael started setting out the *banchan on the informal kitchen table, reserved for casual family dinners*. Once he was done putting out the small plates of accompaniments for the rice, next came the bowls of rice themselves, customized for each person's appetite. Slightly below the rim of the bowl for Mrs. Song and piled in a gentle curve above the rim for James. He couldn't help but smile when Adelaide handed him a bowl, piled high like shaved ice.

"Oh, you remembered," he teased. Maybe they could pretend nothing happened earlier.

"Of course, I remembered. I cook double portions when you and Garrett are around. I'm surprised you guys don't inhale the table." Her tone was light and casual, but she didn't meet his eyes. "Let's go eat."

Although he was distracted by their almost kiss, the home-cooked meal tasted fantastic. It nourished him, body and soul. Michael hoped it carried him through what she had planned for them.

She picked at her food, hardly eating anything at all, and took nervous peeks at her grandmother and him. Michael didn't like that. He didn't like it at all. When she put her spoon down and sipped her water, he tensed for whatever was coming.

*"Hal-muh-nee,"* she said, pausing to clear her throat. "Michael and I wanted to ask your permission to work on a charity event on behalf of Hansol."

He nearly choked on a mouthful of short ribs.

"The two of you? A charity event?" James said, looking back and forth between them.

"*Yoon-ah.*" Mrs. Song usually switched to her grandchildren's Korean names as a sign of affection or when she needed to soften the blow. "I don't think you're—"

"I'm not asking for a permanent position at Hansol. At least not yet," Adelaide interrupted, desperation creeping into her voice. "I know you've been holding me back because I've tarnished our family's reputation before, but this could be my chance to turn that around. A chance to show the public that the youngest of the Songs has her act together."

The eldest Song pressed her lips together with an inscrutable expression. Adelaide took that as her cue to continue. "And I know better than anyone I don't have much hands-on experience. That's why Michael has offered to help."

The water he'd gulped after choking on the short ribs went down the wrong pipe, throwing him into a coughing fit. *What the hell? I offered?* Michael should stop this train wreck but shock and panic rampaged through his mind. He didn't trust himself to be alone with Adelaide for more than a few minutes. There was no way he could spend extended periods of time with her and not slip up.

"Both of you trust and respect Michael, and he *is* our family's PR specialist. He could help me make the right decisions for the charity event, and maximize the chance to rehabilitate my wild-child image."

The table was eerily silent as Mrs. Song gazed down at her folded hands. Then she raised her head with a sigh.

"My reasons for 'holding you back,' as you put it, are not what you think," she said softly. Michael gripped the sides of his chair. Adelaide deserved this chance, and he desperately wanted it for her even though she had chosen the wrong way to get it. "But I think your idea has promise, and your enthusiasm tells me you are determined to succeed."

"Thank you, *Hal-muh-nee.*"

"Don't thank me, yet. I have no intention of helping

you, because this is *your* project and you must succeed
on your own. You're going to have to go through the
proper channels at Hansol to receive the funds to put
together the event. While Michael's guidance would
be appreciated, he could only advise you, not make
your decisions for you." Grace Song's expression grew a
shade harder. "Adelaide, you will be representing Hansol in your endeavors. You must act with utmost professionalism, and I don't want so much as a whiff of
scandal surrounding you while you're working on behalf of Hansol. Remember, the company has a very
proficient CSR department, which is capable of taking
over the event if the need ever arises."

"I won't forget." Adelaide lifted her chin. "I won't
disappoint you and Dad."

James nodded solemnly. "I know you won't, sweetheart."

Michael sat unmoving as his role in the project was
decided for him. He was elated for Adelaide, but she'd
disappointed him by roping him into her project without his permission. His anger rose close to the surface,
replacing his relief and happiness for Adelaide. He'd
known she was spoiled, but this kind of manipulation
was beneath her. He clenched his jaws tight to control
his expression until the elders left the kitchen.

The Song family matriarch had made her decision,
and Michael would not oppose her without good reason. There was definitely good reason to stop this, but
he couldn't tell Mrs. Song he ached to make love to her
granddaughter. Adelaide's goals for charitable work and
repairing her reputation were important to her and her
family. That was precisely why he'd encouraged her to

pursue this. What infuriated him was her complete dis-
regard of his autonomy. Did she think so little of him?

He finished his meal in silence as the Song family
members discussed the charity organizations while they
ate. They were surprised Adelaide had chosen Learn-
Autism as her charity—she'd never mentioned her
interest in autism awareness before—but they were im-
pressed by her passion and knowledge about the cause.
She was animated and excited about the project, but
avoided his eyes throughout the meal.

The elder Songs moved to the family room for macarons and tea, and Liliana followed them with the macaron tower. Michael and Adelaide cleared the table in
silence but when she began pulling on rubber gloves
to do the dishes, he turned her to face him and trapped
her against the sink with his hands planted firmly by
her waist.

"Explain yourself." His voice sounded like a rough
scrape against cement.

Her lashes fluttered in a rare show of nerves. She
knew what she'd done was wrong, but she'd done it
anyway. "You would've said no."

"You're right."

"But why?" Frustration burst out of her without
warning, her face for once an open book. "I don't understand why things have to be so weird between us.
Why can't you help me do this?"

"I would have said no because… I have my reasons.
Besides, the whole point is to prove yourself. Instead,
you used me as a pawn to get your grandmother's approval." He shifted closer, eliminating the gap between

their bodies. "And didn't we discover earlier why things have to be *weird* between us?"

"But…" When he leaned his face closer to hers, she automatically rose up on her toes before she caught herself. "Oh."

He couldn't hold back his chuckle at her crestfallen expression. He leaned back to break the electricity churning between them. "*Oh* is right."

She caught her bottom lip between her teeth, her eyebrows low over her eyes. It was her thinking face. She was freaking adorable, but the next words out of her scared the crap out of him.

"There's this crazy chemistry between us," she said as though she was talking to herself.

"I wouldn't go that far," he quickly replied. Her words made their attraction seem all too real, and that was dangerous. Michael hastily retreated a few steps, but it did nothing to diminish the magnetic pull of their desire.

"Then what would you call it?" She arched an eyebrow at him, crossing her arms over her chest. "Sibling-like affection?"

"Adelaide, just stop this. Whatever it is, we are not going anywhere near that land mine." He wanted to be firm, but he just sounded desperate to his own ears. "Look, I'll find you a good fit from Reynolds PR to work on the project."

She opened her mouth as though to protest, but her reasonable mask slid in place. "That guy Aiden seems nice."

"The point of this charity project is to elevate your public image," he bit out. Aiden had given Adelaide lovesick glances the few times she'd visited Michael at the office. "Pairing you with him would be PR suicide."

"You think I'm going to have a fling with Aiden?" Her head jerked back as though Michael had slapped her. "You think I'm going to risk the most important project of my life to screw one of your employees? That I have so little self-control that I'd put Hansol's reputation at risk?"

"That's not what I meant," he said, his alarm rising as Adelaide crumbled in front of him. Her fear, heartbreak and vulnerability gutted him.

"I thought you and I…we were…" Her chin trembled as her beseeching eyes sought his. But whatever she saw there brought a defensive wall crashing down around her, and all emotion seeped out of her. *No. Please, don't.* "I apologize for misunderstanding our relationship so abysmally. You're right. I shouldn't have tried to rope you into this. I'll do it on my own."

# Three

Hansol's Corporate Social Responsibility Department accepted her proposal for a charity fashion show but allotted her a rather tight budget. Adelaide focused her energy on putting together a design contest for local college students. For the first round, the designers had entered their most recent portfolios, and Adelaide selected the top ten entries. Now for round two, the finalists would form her design team, and create sensory-friendly clothing for the runway. The contest would culminate in the charity fashion show where the grand prize winner would receive a coveted summer internship at Hansol.

"Thank you so much for coming to meet with me today." Adelaide was nervous yet determined as she addressed her ten finalists in their first meeting at Hansol.

She stood at the head of the table in the conference room with a steady tremor in her gut. As she looked out at the eager, excited faces of the student designers, the weight of responsibility settled around her shoulders. This was happening. *Oh, God.* If she failed, they would fail with her, *because* of her.

"I'm sure many of you don't know this, but I majored in fashion design…" Adelaide's words trailed off as a cacophony of protests erupted around the conference table. The room filled with disbelieving laughter.

"Not know?" said a guy who resembled a young lumberjack in his flannel shirt. "I wouldn't be here if I hadn't seen your work in the Cornell Fashion Collective Runway Show."

A lovely brunette with a pixie cut bounced on her chair with her hand raised high in the air. Embarrassed to the tips of her toes, Adelaide quickly pointed at her. "You were the freaking winner of the Cornell Design Award."

"As far as I'm concerned, you weren't born *into* a fashion giant's family. You were born to *be* a fashion designer," said one of the older students. "Just like me. I took a detour to raise three beautiful children, but here I am now."

Adelaide pressed trembling fingers to her mouth to stop a sob. These strangers had more faith in her than her own family and friends. By some miracle, they saw past the spoiled heiress and saw the person she dreamed of becoming. Failure was not an option. She would take these beautiful dreamers and give them wings to fly. She was born into privilege, and it would be *her* privilege to help these talented designers with every advantage in her arsenal.

"Thank you. I'll do everything in my power not to let you down."

Adelaide swallowed the lump in her throat as laughter and applause followed her words. She proceeded to make her presentation on a wave of adrenaline.

"In conclusion, I know it was more than your love of fashion that brought you here today. It is our shared passion to raise autism awareness that will inspire and motivate us to make this charity fashion show one for the ages."

After thundering applause, handshakes and hugs, Adelaide soon found herself in an empty conference room with excitement and energy lingering in the air. She wanted to change for the better not so others would love and accept her, but so she could love and accept herself. Chasing fleeting pleasures and distractions had only hollowed her out more, and she'd grown tired of being a human mash-up of grief, loneliness and loss. She still had a long road to achieving that purpose, but she was proud of how far she'd come.

And she had no right to resent Michael for not wanting to work with her. She'd tried to manipulate him into being part of her project. She owed him an apology for that, but her reasons for seeking Michael's help had not changed. She needed to publicize the event and make connections with bighearted donors, which meant she needed a PR specialist. Hansol and her family trusted Reynolds PR, and that was who she would go with. Michael had plenty of competent employees who would jump at the chance.

If she closed her eyes, Adelaide could still feel the slide of his mouth against her hot skin and his tightly reined desire shaking to break free. His blue eyes had turned nearly black as they'd roamed down her body, and she'd felt a thousand sparks alight on her skin. She'd wanted to climb him and devour his mouth even before he'd touched her.

Adelaide opened her eyes and released a shuddering sigh. *Hell.* She could not have feelings for Michael again. He was wise to be weirded out. What they needed was their friendship back. Not this stilted, impersonal "friendship" they had now, but the one they used to share as kids, where they trusted and cared deeply about each other. Where loyalty was never in doubt.

She slid into a seat near the center of the table, and dialed the Reynolds PR main line on the conference speaker phone. This was business. Calling Michael's cell phone would be unprofessional.

"Reynolds PR. This is Trisha speaking. How may I direct your call?"

"Hi, Trisha. This is Adelaide Song. I need to hire a PR specialist for a charity event I'm organizing for Hansol. This project is independent of Hansol's general business, so I'd rather not pull anyone from the current Hansol team."

"Of course, Ms. Song. I'll connect you to someone who could answer your questions in detail and assign the right specialist for you."

"Perfect. Thanks, Trisha."

Lounge music filled her ears as she waited on hold, swinging from left to right on her wheeled leather chair.

"Ms. Song?" A male voice interrupted the bad Muzac, and she released a breath of relief.

"Who am I speaking with?"

"This is Aiden Lewis."

"Oh… Hello, Aiden." *Great. The very man Michael warned me off of.* Well, it wasn't like she'd asked for him. He was just a point person to assist her for now. "Please call me Adelaide. So has Trisha filled you in on my general needs?"

"Oh, yes." A spark of life entered Aiden's bland voice. "It's fantastic you're heading a charity project. I have specialized experience in that field, so I hope we get a chance to work together."

"Well, I'm sure you need to consider all the details before deciding who's best for the project." Adelaide pinched the bridge of her nose, irritated by the unwanted complication of dealing with Aiden when Michael had told her not to.

"Yes…well. Of course." The man flustered easily. She would bet he was nodding furiously on the other end of the call. "When would be a good time for us to meet? I'll work around your schedule. We could meet for lunch or drinks to discuss the details, if you'd like."

"Why don't I come into your office tomorrow afternoon?" she relented, even though she thought this part could be done over the phone. "Does four o'clock work for you?"

"That. Is. Perfection," Aiden said fervently.

*Oh, jeez.*

"Correct me if I'm wrong." Michael drew a slow breath and fought to dull the murderous edge in his voice. Forcing his fists to unfurl on his desk, he leveled Aiden with a steely gaze. "Are you meeting with one of my longstanding clients without my approval?"

"I thought your client was Hansol Corporation." Aiden cocked his head, his eyes squinted in confusion. "She specifically requested someone not on the Hansol team."

"Either way, you should have run it by me. Hansol Corporation is my client, but my authority isn't confined to one specific team or project. As the head of this company, I oversee every team. Furthermore, I *personally* represent the Song family when the need arises."

"Have you ever represented Adelaide?"

*Adelaide?* Since when had Aiden and she been on a first-name basis?

"No, but *Ms. Song* comes under the umbrella of the Song family," Michael said in a low, icy voice. "You stepped over the line when you booked an appointment with her, knowing who she was. And now you are pushing toward insubordination by challenging my authority to decide who represents my clients."

"I sincerely apologize for not running this by you earlier, but I'm doing so now." Aiden had switched to a diplomatic, placating tone. "I'm clear on Ms. Song being your client by default, but if you're not taking her project on yourself then I would like to volunteer my services."

"Her project entails intimate knowledge of her, her family and Hansol. I'm afraid only I can assist her properly." Michael made a show of checking his watch and pinned Aiden with an arctic glare. "Get back to work. This conversation is over. I need to prepare for a meeting with my client."

* * *

Michael paused a few feet from the entrance to the small meeting room where Adelaide was waiting and stared at her. It wasn't by choice. It was a compulsion. Even though she was Garrett's little sister, he'd always thought Adelaide was beautiful. From an objective point of view. But there was nothing objective about his appraisal now. He drank her in with selfish greed.

She was even more stunning than usual today. Her shapely legs were crossed at the knees and angled to one side. Her short pencil skirt revealed some skin, but her posture ensured that she didn't reveal an inch more than she intended. Her long silky hair fell down one side of her shoulders and he wanted to reach out and touch the cool, midnight strands.

Her makeup was immaculate and matched her shimmery gray suit. Her skin was flawless, her long, full eyelashes fanned like a peacock's tail, and the soft pink stain on her lips looked like what would remain after bloodred lipstick had been kissed off her.

It took Herculean effort to draw in a full breath and clear his face of the lustful expression he knew was there. Michael couldn't unthink the realization that he wanted Adelaide with a fierce desperation. He yearned to taste every part of her. It was screwed up and wrong, but he had to deal with that later.

Adelaide lifted her eyes from her tablet as Michael strode into the meeting room, closing the door behind him. Her pretty little lips parted in surprise and he nearly groaned. Screwed up or not, he had his hands full controlling his reaction to her.

"I'm supposed to be meeting with Aiden. I called the

main line and Trisha transferred me to him, so don't get your panties in a knot." Her voice matched the challenge in her expression. "I didn't come to dig my promiscuous claws into him."

Michael flinched. "I never implied…" His words trailed off as he noticed all the blinds in the meeting room were closed. Aiden must've wanted some privacy. Michael cursed under his breath. "Aiden isn't suited for your project. Plus, he's interested in you, which could be a nuisance down the line."

"I know what you mean. He asked me out for drinks to 'discuss business.' I suggested we meet here instead." Some of the rancor went out of her eyes as she drew her shoulders back. "Michael, I owe you an apology for pulling that childish stunt on you the other night."

He was too relieved that she had rejected Aiden's advances to stay angry. But when he opened his mouth to object that she didn't need to apologize, she pushed on with what sounded like a practiced speech.

"And none of this is about the kitchen incident. I really do need a PR specialist to get the right kind of attention for this project and help with 'rehabilitating' my image." She shrugged her shoulders in a charming, self-deprecating way. "Less party animal, more solid, grounded professional. So will you please find me an amazing specialist?"

Ignoring the sharp twist in his stomach, he forced a half smile. Adelaide wanted to put what had happened behind them. Well, so did he. He wanted nothing more than to forget the troubling moment in the kitchen.

"So you didn't tell your grandmother I was being a big bully?"

"Oh, please. I don't tattle." Her eyes twinkled with mischievous glee when she added, "You could tell her yourself about being a bully and not helping out. She's going to wonder why you assigned someone else to assist me."

"I'm not telling her that."

"Don't be such a chicken. I've come to terms with you not wanting to work with me." Her teasing tone was almost convincing but a flash of hurt darkened her face before she erased all traces of it. "But I'll feel a lot better when *Hal-muh-nee* bites your head off for refusing to help me."

"Or I could tell her you lied to both of us." He played along, enjoying the beginnings of her pout.

"Goddammit, Michael. Can't you just do this one thing for me without rubbing my face in it? We grew up together. Doesn't that count for anything?"

"We didn't exactly grow up together. I'm eight years older than you. It's more accurate to say I helped raise you."

She shifted from being annoyed to pissed off, but he couldn't stop his teasing. Getting a rise out of her was irresistible. He was enjoying the color surging in her cheeks, the stubborn line of her lips and the flash of temper in her eyes. It was intoxicating because he'd broken through the facade she put up for everyone else. In these rare moments, he saw Adelaide without her masks, and he couldn't get enough.

*God. What would she look like if she fell apart in my arms...crying out my name?*

"I...uh..." She blinked rapidly and suddenly seemed unsure. "You're looking at me strangely. Are you angry?

Because I didn't come here to pick a fight with you. I didn't even know we were meeting. Just—let's start over. Hi, I'm Adelaide Song, and I need to hire a PR specialist for my charity event."

"A pleasure to meet you, Ms. Song." He mentally smacked the side of his head. "My name's Michael Reynolds and I'll be assisting you with your event."

Her face went blank with surprise, then lit up with the most blinding smile he'd ever seen. "Really? You're forgiving me? You're going to help?"

"Yes." He gave in to his chuckle, inexplicably proud of himself for making her happy. "I'll do everything in my power to make your charity event a success and shape your image to fit who you are now."

"Thank you, Michael. This means the world to me." With laughter in her eyes, Adelaide reached across the table and gave his hand a squeeze. "It almost makes me want to forgive you for being an overbearing know-it-all. Almost."

Fire lit across his skin at her touch, and the soft smile on her face—a real smile just for him—made him ache to kiss her. He linked his fingers through hers and held on to her gaze until the sexual tension squeezed all the air out of his lungs. He dropped her hand, rounded the table and lifted her up by her arms. She squeaked and pressed her hands against his chest, not quite pushing him away.

He was acting like a madman. What was he planning to do? Kiss her until neither of them could breathe. His lustful, out-of-control answer shook him out of his trance. He carefully relaxed his fingers, then dropped his hands to his sides. It was only when he stepped back that he realized Adelaide's fingers had curled around his lapel. His gaze lowered to her hands and back up to her eyes, and the desire, confusion and hope in them nearly dropped him to his knees.

"Adelaide." Her name was a hoarse plea on his lips, but he didn't know what he was begging for.

"Let's go grab some dinner," she said brightly, moving away from him.

"Sounds good." He cleared the gravel from his throat. "We have a life-changing charity event to pull off."

"You're damn right we do." Her smile was an amalgam of regret and determination. She held out her hand and said in a steel-laced voice, "Here's to our professional relationship."

He took her hand and shook it firmly, sensing the iron railings crash down around her. In an instant, Adelaide was out of his reach.

# Four

Michael would always draw away from her. Seeing her as a woman, as someone he desired, terrified him. Adelaide could see it in his eyes. It probably arose from some misplaced sense of loyalty to Garrett and the rest of the Song clan. Every time his attraction rose to the surface, he drowned himself in guilt and shame. Like he wasn't worthy. *Idiot.*

Even so, she couldn't deny the flash of gratification his attraction brought her. It was small consolation for a decades-long crush, but it was something. She let out a wistful sigh and made another attempt to read over the menu. Finding parking in downtown Los Angeles took more patience than Adelaide possessed at the moment, so they'd strolled to her favorite seafood restaurant a couple blocks from Reynolds PR. One of the small joys of being in DTLA was having incredible eats within walking distance, from food trucks to Michelin-starred restaurants, like the one they were sitting in.

The old-school mahogany decor didn't encourage a romantic mood. Thank goodness for small mercies. She was already overheated from the reluctant, hot glances Michael shot her way. But indulging in her childish hopes for a happily-ever-after would only hurt them both. It was time to put herself out of misery and forget the brief bursts of desire they'd shared. They were old friends, and business associates now. There couldn't be anything more between them.

"Are you ready to order?" Their server filled their wineglasses with precision, then straightened. "Or would you like a few more minutes?"

"We're ready." Adelaide didn't want Michael to guess she was too distracted to read through the menu. She hoped her choice was still on this season's menu. "We'll start with a dozen Kumamoto oysters and littleneck clams, and I'll have a Niçoise salad as my main."

"A lovely choice," he said, then turned toward Michael. "And for you, sir?"

"Um…" His eyes flickered rapidly across the menu, making her bite her cheek to stop a wicked grin from surfacing. She wasn't the only one who was having trouble concentrating. "I'll take the black cod."

"Excellent." With a slight bow of his head, the server slipped away.

Silence hung between them as she fiddled with the silverware and he took a sip of wine. *Oh, this is ridiculous.*

"I've been busy the past few weeks," she blurted a

little louder than necessary. *Stupid nerves.* "I opened a design contest for local college students with a summer internship at Hansol as the grand prize. I already selected ten finalists to be my design team for the charity event."

"You *have* been busy." Michael said, leaning forward in his seat. "How will you choose the winner?"

"The preliminary round was based on their portfolios, but I'll select the winner based on their design contributions to the sensory-friendly evening collection we'll debut at the fashion show."

"You're raising awareness among future designers, as well as the influential guests and consumers. A masterful move," he said with open admiration.

Pride filled Adelaide's heart at his simple praise. He was her friend and his opinion mattered to her. That was all. She gulped down some wine and firmly affixed her business expression. "So when does the PR magic begin?"

"Tonight." He sat back in his seat and crossed his arms over his chest. "I'll compile a strategic guest list, including the usual fashion icons, philanthropists, lifestyle bloggers and whoever else necessary to peg the fashion show as an A-list event. Then tomorrow…"

When he didn't continue right away, she prompted him impatiently. "Tomorrow what? What happens tomorrow?"

"Well, starting tomorrow, I need to smile, charm and grovel to get as many of them to attend as possible."

Adelaide burst out laughing. "You? Groveling? I've got to see that."

"Do you, now?" A sly glint entered his eyes, which

sent a frisson of excitement down her spine. "You could witness it firsthand…as you grovel right alongside me."

"What? That's your job. I've got my hands full planning every last detail of the actual event."

"I'll help where I can with the preparations, but I need to grovel in person to convince a few of the big guns to attend, and I need the Hansol heiress there with me. It'll make them feel extra special."

"Fine." She rolled her eyes and mimed a subtle gag, but he was absolutely right. "I'll go butt kissing with you."

"Thank you for your gracious consent." His grin turned a little wicked. "If you need to practice beforehand, I'd be happy to assist you."

"Are you saying I should kiss your cute behind?" Because she would really, really like to kiss it, grab it, bite it and spank—she put a full stop on the horny train of thought. Michael's smile slipped a notch, and his eyes narrowed dangerously. *Gulp.* He looked like he wanted to…spank her. *Backtrack, backtrack!*

She sighed in relief when Michael shook his head as though to clear it. Disaster avoided. Adelaide couldn't believe herself. She had come to a firm decision not to cross the friendship line, and she'd slipped up five minutes later.

"Tell me what you're envisioning for the event," he said, bringing their conversation back on topic.

"The fashion show and auction, where the guests get to bid on their favorite pieces, are the main event. I'm also working on an overall visual theme for the venue that'll leave a lasting impression."

"Why does that make me nervous?" He gave her a crooked grin to accompany his half joke.

"Because jolly ol' Mike becomes a stick-in-the-mud when it comes to me." Adelaide managed to keep the bitterness out of her voice. *Water under the bridge and all that.* If she wanted to rid their friendship of any *weirdness* and work well with him, she had to focus on the here and now. "But, seriously, do yourself a favor and stop with the babysitter role. You don't have any heightened duty to hover over me. Just treat me like one of your friends. We *are* friends, right?"

"Of course, we're friends," he said, a line deepening between his brows.

"Good."

They were on the same wavelength. There would be nothing more than friendship between them. It was for the best.

Still…as their food arrived, a corner of Adelaide's heart grew cold, as though a warm campfire flickered and died away inside her.

The next day in the studio, Chris, the sad-eyed lumberjack, in one of his endless plaid shirts, came to stand beside her. When he didn't say anything, Adelaide glanced up from the sketch she'd been studying. He was thoughtfully rubbing his beard with his eyes focused on his design.

"It's missing something," he said.

"Mmm-hmm." She didn't pretend to misunderstand him. The floor-length gown was on trend, and would sell well at any department store, but it wasn't a design that captured her attention like his portfolio had. "It's beautiful, but…"

"It leaves me cold. I don't see much of myself in it."

"Why did you enter the contest?" Adelaide knew many of the contestants had entered for a chance to intern at Hansol, but her gut instinct told her there was more to it where Chris was concerned.

"My kid brother's on the spectrum," he said with a helpless shrug. "He's so smart, kind and funny, but he faces so many challenges dealing with everyday life. I feel helpless sometimes, because I can't make everything better for him. This contest gave me a chance to do more. For him and others with ASD."

"So you have special insight into what people with autism might want or need."

"Well, I know what my brother likes and dislikes."

"Then design something your brother would love to wear."

"But he's only nine. I thought we were focusing on business and formal wear."

"You could design business and formal wear based on what you think your brother might like to wear when he's older." Chris's gaze drifted into space, as though an idea had sparked to life.

"Thank you," he said in a faraway voice, and carefully withdrew his sketch from her desk.

She smiled as he hastened back to his workspace. The creative energy in their makeshift studio was manic. Adelaide couldn't remember the last time she'd sketched out so many ideas in one sitting.

The company had cleared out a large sample room for her and her team. She had five individual desks set up with an oversize table in the center of the room. Everyone came in when they had time, so the studio held five to six people at any given moment. If all ten designers showed up at once then they might need an additional oxygen source.

"I like your office."

Adelaide bounced in her seat when the deep, familiar voice reached her ears. She swiveled around to find Michael grinning down at her. *No, it's Mike, not Michael.* Calling him Michael had been her secret way to express her feelings out loud. Growing up, he was her guardian angel. He was by her side through the roughest times, and always knew how to make her feel better. Kind, gentle, vulnerable and sweet Michael. *Her* Michael…but no more.

"Hey, Mike." She stood up so she wouldn't have to tilt her head back like a Pez dispenser to look at his face. "What are you doing here?"

"Hmm." A frowned creased his smooth forehead, but his voice remained light. "That's not very hospitable. I *am* a member of your event team after all."

"That's true," she conceded, and ground her heel into the burst of joy brought on by his sudden appearance. "Welcome then."

"Any luck finding a venue for the show?" he asked casually.

"None." She sighed, her shoulders sagging. "I don't want to spend half of my budget on the venue, which means my choices are limited at best."

"Well, I have good news for you. A friend of mine has a loft studio in the arts district, and he owes me a favor."

* * *

Everyone called him Mike.

He had no idea he hated the nickname until Adelaide made the switch. She'd always called him Michael, and he'd loved the sound of his name rolling off her sweet tongue. But now he was *Mike*, her friend. Dull, bland and impersonal. He absolutely hated it.

"A loft in the arts district?" Her eyes lit up with excitement.

"Yes, with lots of natural light and open space." He felt his lips turn up at the corners. Mike or not, making her happy made him feel a hundred feet tall. "With a standard runway, it should seat about a hundred-fifty guests."

"That sounds too good to be true. How much is he asking for it?" She narrowed her eyes at him.

"A thousand dollars even."

"Per day?"

"Nope. For the entire duration, including setup and clean-up time."

"No freaking way," she whispered. "That's a full week. For a thousand."

"Yes, it is. And you're welcome." His reluctant smile grew into a full-blown grin. "But you need to come with me right now. He's leaving for San Francisco tonight and won't be back for a few days. You probably want to check the venue off the to-do list as soon as possible, right? We'll finally have a set date and location."

Her dazed eyes snapped to focus, and she gathered her purse and rummaged around her cluttered desk until she found her iPad. "Let's go."

Most of her design team was too busy to notice her

leaving, but she waved to the couple of them who looked up when she and Michael passed.

"Whose car are we taking?" she asked as they stepped into the elevator.

"Yours." He'd walked over from his office. It was several blocks away, but he needed to stretch his legs. Adelaide could give him a ride back to his office later. He ignored the small voice that told him he was scavenging for a precious few extra minutes with her.

"Okay," she said, unaware of his ulterior motives.

Michael cleared his throat several times. "I'll drive, though, since I know the way."

"Sounds good."

He hadn't seen her in days, and standing next to her was heady. She was wearing a silky cream dress shirt with a pair of slim black slacks and red oxfords. Her outfit was professional, and still functional enough to allow her to do the legwork for the event. But all he could see was how unbelievably beautiful she looked. The soft fabric of her shirt clung to the tops of her breasts and flowed loosely over her torso to where it was tucked into her slacks.

She tossed him her car keys as they approached her car, and he caught them by instinct. Adelaide slid into the passenger side, and Michael folded himself into the driver's seat with a grunt. The auto adjust allowed him to inch the seat back and slowly lower his knees from his chest.

"I sometimes forget how short you are," he said with a scowl. Adelaide was gripping her sides, hunched over in laughter. "It's a wonder you don't need a wooden block tied to your foot to reach the pedals."

"Shut up and drive, Gulliver."

They settled into a comfortable silence that came from years of friendship, and he clung to the familiar feeling. LA's arts district was being gentrified, but it still hung on to its bohemian roots. Rough slashes of graffiti shared walls with stunning murals by professional artists, and ramshackle hole-in-the-wall restaurants stood between updated condos and art galleries. The eclectic but well-balanced vibe made for inspired wine and art walks, which took place every few weeks.

His friend's loft was on the top floor of one of the buildings housing an art gallery. The bright red exterior stood out like a bright jewel on the street. He circled the building five times before he found street parking.

Adelaide shot out of her seat before he could open her door for her. He sighed and stepped out of the car. She usually snorted at his efforts at chivalry anyway.

"You must be joking." Her jaw hung slack. "The meter doesn't take cards. Who carries around a sack of quarters these days?"

Michael shrugged. He rarely used cash, and when he did he always left a tip, including any coins he got back as change. "There's a Vietnamese restaurant across the street. Let's grab something to drink for all of us, and get a sack of quarters."

"Ooh. I'd kill for some iced Vietnamese coffee right now."

"No murderous rampage necessary," he said with a wink. "See? We're already here."

"Table for two?" One of the waitstaff approached them when they went inside.

"No, we're not staying," Adelaide said quickly.

"Could we get three iced coffees to go please? Oh, and some change in quarters."

"No snacks for the road? Some spring rolls maybe?"

"Um…" She pursed her lips, clearly tempted by the suggestion.

"It's probably not a good idea to have your hands and mouth full while you tour the venue," Michael said. "But we could come back for dinner if you'd like."

"Ooh. Good plan." She rubbed her hands together, smiling gleefully. God, she was adorable. "No spring rolls. Just coffee for now."

"Sure. Let me put that order in and I'll be right back to ring you up."

When their server walked away, Adelaide grabbed a menu from the counter. "Jackpot. They have *banh xeo*."

"I don't think I've tried that before." He peeked over her shoulder and glanced at the color picture on the menu. "It kind of looks like an omelet."

"It's actually this thin, crispy crepe filled with your choice of filling like pork, shrimp and bean sprouts. I rarely see it on menus, so I'm super excited. I hope they don't disappoint."

"It's our signature dish. I promise you won't be disappointed," the server said with a kind smile.

"I'm so sorry." Adelaide turned pink and fidgeted beside him like she'd been caught with her hand in the tip jar fishing for a penny. "I didn't mean to be disrespectful. I'm sure they'll be lovely and I'll eat like seven of them."

"Please." The server waved aside her apology. "I was only teasing. But I wasn't kidding about the *bahn xeo*. It's my grandmother's recipe, and you won't find its equal anywhere."

"Wow. I can't wait to come try some."

Michael grinned at the exchange and pulled out a twenty to pay for their coffee only to have Adelaide slap his hand away.

"I got it."

"Hell, no," he said, blocking her attempt to pay. "You're going to buy me dinner after you sign for the venue."

Adelaide's laughter enveloped him like the lovely strains of a violin. "Fair enough."

With a tray of iced coffee in his hands and a pocket full of quarters, they crossed the street to her car. When he transferred the drink holder to one hand to reach for some quarters, the coffee wobbled dangerously with the uneven distribution of weight.

"Stop." She spoke with such urgency that Michael froze on the spot. "Don't you dare spill my Vietnamese coffee. Hang tight to those and I'll get the quarters."

A blinking red alarm went off in his head. But before he could shove the drinks at her and get the coins himself, Adelaide's warm, small hand slid into his pocket. *God.* He didn't know where the strength had come from, but he held in the desperate groan that filled his throat.

Her hand stilled in his pocket as though she was just now realizing what she was doing. Looking intently at the meter, she swept her hand in a giant, scooping motion and withdrew a small mountain of quarters. The good thing was she seemed to have harvested enough coins to not go in for a second time. The bad—and wonderful—thing was she'd managed to caress his taut thigh, forcing him to recite the alphabet backward in his head.

"Okay." She cleared her throat and captured his gaze head-on, as if she was daring him to make things awkward. "Let's go see this miraculous venue you found for us."

Needing to walk behind her as he got his pants under control, he handed the drinks over. "Why don't you carry these and offer him the coffee as a bribe?"

She took the tray, rolling her eyes. He opened the door for Adeleaide and they began climbing the back stairs to the loft. Unfortunately, walking behind her and watching her round backside rise and fall didn't help with his hard on situation. He resolutely stared down at the steps and nearly bumped into her when they reached the fourth floor.

"Dude. Respect the *coffee*," she said, steadying the drink holder.

"Sorry. I was lost in my thoughts," he mumbled as he reached around her to open the door to the loft.

"Were you thinking about the *bahn xeo*, too? I'm so hungry right now."

A huff of laughter escaped him. "Exactly. I can't stop thinking about the *bahn xeo*."

"Mike." Glen, his college buddy, strode across the loft and pulled him in for a bro hug, complete with chest bump and robust back thumping. "It's good to see you, man."

"Glen, this is Adelaide Song, the producer of Hansol's charity fashion show," he said, finally comfortable enough to glance in her direction. "Adelaide, this is Glen, photographer extraordinaire and the owner of this loft."

"Nice to meet you." She handed the drinks to Michael, and extended her hand for a handshake.

"The pleasure's mine," Glen replied, taking her hand and covering it with both of his. "Mike gave me a brief sketch of what you're planning, and I greatly admire your efforts."

Glen held on to her hand two seconds longer than necessary, propelling Michael into action. "Why don't you two grab your coffee, so I can put this tray down."

"Is this Vietnamese iced coffee from across the street? I love that restaurant, especially this drink. Thanks, man."

"Don't thank me." Michael deposited the drink tray in the recycling bin and turned toward her with his coffee in his hand. "Adelaide's trying to bribe you."

"Thanks, Adelaide. But I was sold the moment you walked in," Glen said with a wink.

She laughed good-naturedly but didn't respond to his friend's flirting. *Good*. Because the back of his neck was hot and scratchy, and he had to fight his caveman impulse to plant his palm on her behind and pull her up against him. *Mine*.

"How about a quick tour?" she said, glancing around the loft.

The three of them walked through the space and admired the three-sixty view the surrounding windows provided. The setting sun added a warm hue to the white walls and walnut floors. They certainly could use the ambience and clean palette to their advantage in the fashion show.

"Of course, all the furniture and photography equipment will be cleared out for you," his friend explained.

Adelaide held up a finger, her expression growing thoughtful. She paced a few steps back and forth, then clapped her hands together. "Thank you, and your setup here just gave me a great idea. I think it'll be fantastic to have a photo opportunity for the guests. They could choose which set they want to be in and be captured like a model in a magazine."

"That's a fantastic idea," Glen said.

"We could put together one photo booth with extra bright lights and loud music for the guests to experience how a typical setup with lights and music might feel for people with autism," she went on. "And include a set with muted lights and music to allow any guests on the spectrum to participate as well."

Michael was so proud of her, but he couldn't spin her off the ground like he wanted to in front of Glen. Instead, he pulled her into light, friendly hug, and whispered before he stepped back, "You're amazing. Do you know that?"

"Yeah, I know." Her shy smile and lovely blush belied her cocky words.

"It sounds like we have a deal," Michael said to his friend, not taking his eyes off Adelaide.

"But a thousand dollars for an entire week? That is much too generous," she protested.

"I've changed my mind about that." Glen paused for effect. He'd always loved hamming it up. "I would love for you to use the loft free of charge."

"No, that's too much," Adelaide gasped.

Michael grinned and fist-bumped his friend. "You're

still one of the good guys. I'm glad all that drinking in college didn't mess up your brain."

"But—"

"Adelaide," Glen said. "I love your enthusiasm and passion for your cause, and you've convinced me to do my part to help."

"Well, damn. I don't know what to say, Glen," she said, excitement bubbling to the surface. "Thank you. I guess the Vietnamese coffee worked like a charm."

"Yup. That must be it," Michael's friend replied with a robust guffaw.

Adelaide had always been amazing with people, but her passion for the charity made her a force to be reckoned with. They sealed the deal, disposing of the necessary contract with efficient professionalism, and everyone said their goodbyes with wide grins.

A new moon hung high in the sky by the time they strolled back to her car, but Adelaide was oblivious to her surroundings. Her hands were clasped in front of her chest and she looked blinding in her joy. He wanted to steal a taste of her sweet faraway smile.

"I still can't believe we scored that venue." Her whisper rose to a squeal on the last word. "It's perfect."

"It must feel great to check that huge box off your list," Michael said a little stiffly, giving himself a firm mental shake. Her undiluted joy and sweetness weren't his to take.

"It really does. Now I can finally get started with everything else." She placed a hand on his arm before they crossed the street for *banh xeo*. "Thank you, Mike."

*Mike.* Her heartfelt thanks should've warmed him,

but the distance she wedged between them by using the nickname spread ice through his veins.

He should be glad. If she'd reciprocated his desire, he wouldn't have been able to resist her much longer. He was a man of principle, but he was no saint. It wouldn't have mattered that she was his best friend's little sister, and the cherished and overprotected baby of the closest people he had to a family. He would've succumbed if she'd wanted him, too. But she didn't. She was past the fluke in the kitchen the other night.

He should be grateful he wouldn't break the trust of people he cared so much about. He should be relieved. But the wall she'd built around herself made him feel more alone than ever.

# Five

Adelaide dragged herself to work after a few hours of restless sleep. She wished she had one of those beer hats that folks wore to ball games, so she could prop two cups of venti coffee in it. Then again, putting two small buckets of steaming hot liquid on her head probably wasn't the best idea she'd had. In fact, her exhausted brain seemed capable only of spewing gibberish and stupid ideas.

Perhaps the stupidest idea running through her mind was to call Michael even though they didn't have a single meeting on the calendar. She felt the urge to ask him to lunch to brainstorm over the marketing status, or to go over the guest list one more time.

"Coffee," she mumbled as she passed Cindy, the spunky designer with a pixie cut.

"Late night?" The other woman grinned suggestively.

"Lots of work."

Back at her desk with a double espresso, Adelaide dropped her head in her hands and groaned. Suddenly remembering she wasn't alone, she peeked around the studio between her fingers. *Good.* No one was paying her any attention. Her cell vibrated next to her espresso, and she reached for it with more urgency than warranted. It was Michael. Her heart beat a fancy drum solo.

Michael's text was simple. Hey.

Hey, she responded.

I got us an in with Mateo Sanchez.

Adelaide couldn't believe it. Shut. Up.

Mateo Sanchez. He was a renowned director who had a reputation for creating movies featuring people of color in a realistic light. He was a powerful voice for underrepresented groups in the US. Having his support could catapult the charity event and autism awareness beyond anything she'd hoped for.

No, you shut up, Michael shot back.

Real mature, Adelaide typed, grinning at her phone.

Michael wouldn't quit. You started it.

Why are we bickering like we're six? We have an in with Mateo Sanchez! Tell me everything.

Not much to tell. A client knows someone who knows Sanchez's agent. We get ten mins with the agent.

The agent? Not Sanchez?

You're cute. Of course, the agent. Lory Diaz.

When? Where?

Today at 12:30 in West Hollywood.

Where are you? Should we drive together or meet there?

It's 11:00. We have plenty of time.

Stop being so damn calm and tell me where the hell you are. I want to be there right now.

Bossy. I'm downstairs in the lobby. Come on down.

She looked down at her outfit: a cream sleeveless mock-neck and a black pencil skirt with a blue skinny belt, stilettos and a giant tote. That would do.

"Mateo Sanchez," she shouted into the room in general as she clacked toward the exit. "Might get him on the guest list."

"What the..."

"Good luck."

"Mateo Freaking Sanchez?"

Letting the words of encouragement recede in the distance, Adelaide made a dash for the elevators, got off at the lobby with impatience simmering inside, then stopped dead in her tracks. Michael was leaning against a wall, scrolling through his phone. *Hell.* He was sex personified. He wore a black shirt, sleeves rolled up to his elbows, and dark blue slacks that hugged his thighs and no doubt his delectable behind like a fitted glove.

"What are you standing around for?" She sounded out of breath, but hopefully he'd think it was from rushing down to the lobby. "Let's go. Your car. I'm too nervous to drive."

"You. Nervous? I don't believe it." His boyish grin made him look like the Michael she knew growing up, and she wanted to kiss the hell out of him.

"Well, nervous is a bit of an exaggeration. I'm…distracted." By the opportunity to secure Mateo Sanchez's support and by the handsome man walking beside her in the parking structure.

She breathed in deeply and blew out her nerves with her next breath. The man beside her was her old friend, who just happened to be unfairly gorgeous. She was human, so she noticed stuff. Like hot men. It didn't mean she had feelings for him.

Adelaide slid into the passenger seat and turned to him. "So what have you got? How are we going to woo this agent?"

"I'm leaving that part up to you," he said as he backed out of the parking spot. "You have a way with people that's better than any mountain of intel on Sanchez I can provide."

"A way with people?" She snorted with disbelief and ignored the pride fluttering in her heart. "That's a pretty excuse for not doing your homework, Reynolds. Why don't you just say your dog deleted your notes with its big brown nose?"

"I don't have a dog."

"Exactly," she said, arching her brow for good measure when he glanced at her.

"According to the GPS, we have a forty-five-minute drive ahead of us. That gives us plenty of time to prepare a spiel for the meeting." He kept his eyes on the road but lifted a hand to stop her from interrupting. "I'm not kidding. You need to be yourself, and tell Lory why LearnAutism and the fashion show are so important for the community and society as a whole. I'm pretty sure she sees a nauseating amount of plastic smiles and listens to endless prepared speeches. Give her something real and she'll get you Sanchez."

"Do you... Do you really believe that?" Adelaide whispered, feeling a moment of doubt.

The person he was describing was not only a grown woman but a smart, competent one. Was he finally seeing the real her? Had he let go of the helpless little girl in his mind and accepted her for who she was right now? Because that would be a game changer. A life changer.

"Absolutely," he said without hesitation.

Her breath caught and her throat worked to swallow. *He sees me. He believes in me.*

"Well, then," she said unable to hold back her joyous smile. "I won't let you down."

The honking of the oncoming car jolted Michael's attention back to the road and the stop sign he'd almost run. He couldn't look away from her. From her smile. The vulnerable light in her eyes.

The driver behind him leaned on his horn. After almost running the stop sign, Michael hadn't resumed driving, forcing the other car to pass him. He needed to get it together if they were going to arrive in West Hollywood in one piece.

"Sorry," he said, stealing a glance at her. His voice sounded like two boulders being ground into pebbles. He cleared his throat. "And I know you'd never let me down, but more importantly, you won't let yourself down. This charity event is important to you in so many ways. You'll do a fantastic job."

"Thank you," she said again a little breathlessly.

Michael snapped his eyes back to the road and focused on getting his heart into a lower gear. The air was charged with anticipation, and they spent the rest of the ride discussing her pitch.

He valeted his car in front of a fiercely modern café with a stark black, white and red motif. Lory Diaz had chosen the meeting place. Their trendy meeting spot worried him. Would Sanchez's agent be too chic and cool to be interested in what they had to say?

"Wow, I think all the edges in this place could cut me to shreds if I'm not careful," Adelaide quipped as they went inside. "Do you think their mugs are rectangular? And black, of course."

He chuckled and leaned down toward her as he led them to the counter. "Look to your left."

"Oh, my gosh." She muffled her laugh behind her hand. "The mug is a black rectangle. I was totally messing around. This place is so cringey."

"Ms. Song?" came a warm voice from behind them.

Adelaide turned around with a smile, then shot Michael a confused gaze.

"This is Ms. Diaz," he whispered in her ear.

She blushed a bright pink, but schooled her expression to reflect impeccable professionalism. "Ms. Diaz, I didn't expect to see you so soon."

"Neither did I. I came a little early for a much-needed coffee break. I recognized you because I've seen your pictures on social media," she said, shaking Adelaide's hand. "It's a pleasure to meet you. You're even lovelier in person. And you must be Mr. Reynolds. You're a very persistent man."

"Thank you," he replied with a broad grin. He'd been worried by her choice of café, but she gave off a good vibe. "And please call me Mike."

Returning his smile, she said, "You two are really early. I was hoping to get here before you guys did."

"We thought we'd settle in and wait for you so we didn't waste a minute of your time," Adelaide said, her blush finally fading.

"Why don't we order our drinks and sit at that table by the window?"

"Sounds good." Michael motioned for Lory to order so he could pay for her coffee. "We're still deciding."

A few minutes later, they gathered around the table with their respective drinks in their hands. Michael and Adelaide's regular-sized coffees were served in the black rectangular mugs they'd noticed before, but Lory's large coffee was in a shockingly skinny and tall red oval mug.

"This place is ridiculous, but it's close to my office and their coffee is incredible," Lory said with a teasing smile, confirming their fear she might've overheard them.

"Sorry about that, but I do think they're a little over-the-top." Adelaide laughed sheepishly. "But I'm totally with you about their coffee. Good stuff."

"Even though we're early, we could go until 12:50 p.m. as planned." She glanced down at her watch and said, "Okay...*go*."

He and Adelaide blinked, then stared at each other until Lory snorted.

"That was my idea of a joke, but we do have to end at precisely 12:50. Please, tell me about your charity event."

Relieved laughter broke the ice for them, and Michael watched as the tension left Adelaide's shoulders and she launched her spiel. She was her charming, passionate self as she spoke of autism awareness and the need for sensory-friendly clothing, and how she wanted Hansol to be part of the small movement happening across the country, bringing its own angle and resources to the growing industry.

"There's a real need for well-designed clothing for adults with autism. Plenty of people on the spectrum are successful professionals and need to dress appropriately. But suits and dresses, with their buttons, zippers, rough seams and scratchy fabrics can really trigger discomfort and not everyone can afford to have their clothes custom-made. Currently, the choices are limited. One—be wealthy. Two—stick with whatever comfortable clothing is out there, even if it's not appropriate for the occasion. Or three—wear business and formal clothes and suck it up, even if they make you want to crawl out of your skin. I want to change that, because those aren't real choices."

A contemplative expression crossed Lory's face before she nodded firmly. "Adelaide, Mateo is going to want to meet you. And soon."

Adelaide gasped, and Michael sat forward with excitement. "We'll fit our schedule around his. Just let us know the time and place. We'd be honored to speak with Mr. Sanchez."

Lory looked at her watch again and smiled apologetically at them. "That sounds great. We need to stop now, but I'll definitely be in touch. Thank you again, and I wish you all the best."

They stepped out into the sun and shook hands before parting ways. As soon as Lory turned the corner, Michael pulled Adelaide into his arms.

"You were amazing," he said, breathing in the intoxicating scent of her hair. "Congratulations."

"We're not done, yet."

Despite her modest words, she clung to him as she trembled with excitement, and he held her, soaking up her elation, unable to let go.

# Six

Adelaide's head was floating above the clouds. As Lory promised, Mateo Sanchez wanted to meet her. At his home in Bel Air. It was a rare privilege. She parked in front of the house after going through the security gates, and surveyed the Mediterranean mansion with interest as she approached the imposing front door. She rang the doorbell and was pleasantly surprised by its quiet, subtle chime.

"Ms. Song," a man in faded jeans and a T-shirt greeted her at the door. "Please come in. I'm Mateo Sanchez."

"Thank you so much for having me." It was the man himself. Just Mateo Sanchez in casual clothes and flip-flops. "And please call me Adelaide."

"Only if you call me Mateo," he said as he led her

through the house. "Would you like a cocktail or some iced tea?"

"Iced tea sounds lovely."

The interior of the mansion was all warm earthy tones and clean-cut elegance. It was huge yet comfortable. Like a home people really lived in. Mateo's kitchen was a space made for entertaining—small dinners, wine parties, casual get-togethers. It somehow also felt perfect for their two-person meeting. He handed her a tall glass of iced tea and sat across from her at the island holding a glass of his own.

"Lory told me about the charity fashion show, and I admire you for your vision and dedication."

"Thank you. There needs to be less othering and more acceptance of people with autism. With the sensory-friendly fashion show, I have the opportunity to spread autism awareness. I hope you can become a part of this important cause, too."

"I'd be happy to attend the event and help the cause in any way, but I also have an ulterior motive for asking you to visit my home," he said, while typing something into his phone.

Adelaide's heart jumped—Mateo Sanchez was coming to the fashion show—then fell to her stomach. She was ecstatic he would be attending, but she wasn't sure about the "ulterior motive" part. *Should I get my pepper spray out?* But Mateo didn't give off any creepy vibes. Before she could ask what his "ulterior motive" involved, a striking teenage girl strode into the kitchen, capturing her attention.

"Stella, this is Adelaide Song, the designer I told you

about," he said, waving the girl toward them. "Adelaide, this is Stella, my daughter."

"Nice to meet you." Adelaide stood and extended her hand to Stella, but the girl's lips turned down at the corners and she drew back. Had Adelaide somehow offended her?

"I'm so happy to meet you, too, Ms. Song," she said, hiding her hands behind her back. "Sorry for not shaking your hand. It's the weirdest custom. The joining of two sweaty, sticky hands, which results in the exchange of bacteria and viruses. I mean, why?"

The puzzle pieces began fitting together. Adelaide's eyes shot to meet Mateo's.

"Stella, may I?" he said.

"Sure." The girl shrugged. "I mean, we can't get to the point of this meeting without telling her."

"Right. Adelaide, my daughter's on the spectrum."

"Thank you for sharing with me," she said simply. There was nothing beyond that to say. "But Mateo, in terms of the charity event, I think you have yet to reveal your 'ulterior motive.'"

"Actually, Stella will discuss that part with you."

Adelaide glanced at Stella with her brows raised, intrigued by this father-daughter tag team.

"So." The teenager lowered her lanky form onto the stool beside her. "I'm turning fifteen in like ten days, and as you probably know, in the Mexican culture, the fifteenth birthday is kind of a big deal. I told my dad that I didn't want a quinceañera because wearing some uncomfortable ball gown all night is what I would call torture, not a party."

The last piece of the puzzle clicked into place and

Adelaide knew what she had to do. "Well, not all ball gowns have to be torture devices. I bet I could create a sensory-friendly gown that would let you dance all night long with minimal discomfort."

"That's what my dad said, but I'm not sure—"

"Tell me," Adelaide interrupted, too excited to stay silent. "Tell me everything that bothers you about clothes, and I'll find a way around them all."

*Holy Mother of God.*

Adelaide was invited to Stella Sanchez's quinceañera, and of course, Michael volunteered to be her plusone. She greeted him at the door of the Song residence in Pacific Palisades wearing a one-shouldered white dress that hugged her body and draped artfully to the floor. She looked stunning. Breathtaking. He literally could not breathe. Then she glided toward him as though she were floating on air.

Maybe he was seeing things as an effect of lack of oxygen in his brain. *Hell.* That meant all his blood was heading south where it didn't belong. He adjusted his tie and thought about swimming in frigid waters.

"You look lovely, Adelaide," he said. He was proud he managed to form coherent words. And was she wearing a new perfume? *God, she's trying to kill me.*

She glanced up and down his body before meeting his eyes. Then she whispered in a husky voice, "You don't look half-bad yourself."

Michael grinned wolfishly, loving the effect he had on her. The more time he spent with this grown-up Adelaide, the more he wanted her. More than he'd ever wanted another woman. Her confidence, intelligence and sense of humor had him entranced.

Wanting more was dangerous. If Mrs. Song found out that he was seeing Adelaide, he couldn't imagine the betrayal she would feel. She had entrusted him with helping Adelaide, not putting her reputation at risk. Besides, she knew his secret. Grace Song was an honorable woman, but she became a mama bear when it came to Adelaide. She wouldn't want a man like him for her granddaughter.

"So is your dress a hit with Stella?" he asked, not liking where his thoughts were headed.

"I don't know yet. She was so quiet during the fitting I couldn't tell what she was thinking." Adelaide fidgeted with her fingers, and Michael gave them a quick squeeze before withdrawing his hand. It burned from the small touch.

"You did an amazing job, and I know how much thought you put into it. Stella has to love it."

"Thanks, Mike." He nearly flinched at the nickname, but he reminded himself it was for the best.

"You're very welcome." He took a deep breath and forced a smile. "That's what friends are for, right?"

"Right," she said with her own sad excuse for a smile.

Michael realized then that she disliked their situation as much as he did. He quelled the pounding of his heart. She had to keep her eyes on the goal, and he had to help her reach that goal.

Their drive out to Bel Air took about twenty minutes, but it felt like hours. Whatever her new scent was, it was driving him crazy; and the damn dress had a slit high up her thigh that revealed creamy skin only a few inches away from his hand. Despite his resolve, her proximity chipped away at his willpower piece by piece.

He breathed in and out through his nose to prevent his blood from rushing south, and stole a glance at Adelaide. With her head turned toward the city lights outside her window, she seemed worlds away. Thank goodness for small blessings, because his trigger-happy dick and slim pants were out to humiliate him.

Artichokes. He should think about artichokes. What was it with people and their love affair with the pine cone–shaped vegetable? *You get a teeth-scrape's worth of the mushy flesh for every tiny leaf, only to reach the heart after all that effort to find it tastes just like a giant kernel of corn.* He would rather eat corn without half the trouble.

His loathing for artichoke hearts distracted him enough to be presentable by the time they reached the Sanchez mansion. When they drove up the driveway, the valet opened Adelaide's door, so Michael got out and went around to tuck her arm into the crook of his arm.

"Shall we?" he said with a formal bow, and waggled his eyebrows. He needed the security of their usual banter to get through the night in one piece.

"Jeez, old man." She snorted. "I think you've watched *The King and I* one too many times."

She was humming "Shall We Dance" under her breath, but stopped with a soft gasp when they arrived at the front entrance.

He didn't need to ask what caused her surprise. Mateo Sanchez's home was impressive on the outside, but the inside was aglow with tiny globes of light in what looked like an enchanted forest. Garlands of vines and ferns, and thick, gnarled trees were entwined with the lights, and a harp's otherworldly strands infused the mist swirling on the floor.

"Oh, man. That lucky girl," Adelaide whispered. "And the lights are perfectly muted and the music is so subtle and gentle, it must put Stella's sensitivities at ease. This is ingenious. No one would dare remark that this sensory-friendly approach is in anyway *less*. Comes in handy to have an amazing director as her dad."

"It does feel magical and Zen. I could get used to living in an enchanted forest," he said as they walked deeper into the most impressive quinceañera he'd ever attended.

"Adelaide!" A beautiful young girl in a silky pearlescent gown screeched to a stop three feet from Adelaide. "Thank you so much for coming. I would never have had this perfect night if it weren't for you."

"You deserve it, Stella. You deserve it all. Never forget that."

"Adelaide." Mateo Sanchez walked up to their group. "We're so glad you could make it."

"Are you kidding? I wouldn't have missed it for the world." She laughed, giving him a warm hug. "Mateo, this is Michael Reynolds, the head of Reynolds PR. He's overseeing the fashion show, and it was his tenacity that made our meeting possible."

"Well, then, I owe Mr. Reynolds my deepest gratitude," he said, extending his hand.

"I've actually come to thank you for your generous support of the fashion show." Michael shook the other man's hand firmly.

"This certainly is a night with a lot to be thankful

for," Sanchez said. "And if you'll excuse us, it's time for our father-daughter dance. Are you ready, Stella?"

"No, but since you've agreed to do away with all the other obligatory dances, I'll have to live with this one," the birthday girl said glumly, unaware that her unfiltered words could be hurtful to her father.

"Ah, as frank as ever." Mateo smiled with pride and a glistening of tears, acknowledging Stella's challenges, and loving her just as she was. "Let's go then, sweetheart."

The father-daughter dance was reminiscent of its counterpart at a wedding. Poignant and heart wrenching. But what moved the crowd the most was the Sanchezes' letter to their daughter, acknowledging her as a grown woman and urging her forward in life with love and respect. Adelaide sniffled beside Michael and he put his arm around her shoulders, bringing her close. She turned to him with a wobbly smile and held his gaze as if to say something, but the crowd erupted in applause when the Sanchezes finished reading the letter and the moment was over.

As the soft strains of the string orchestra flowed through the dance floor again, Michael slid his hand down Adelaide's arm and planted his hand firmly on her back.

"Let's get some air," he whispered, his lips close to her ear.

At her nod, he led them through the balcony doors and into the secluded garden. The half-moon shone brightly in the night sky, and small lampposts dotted the narrow trails lighting their way. He linked his fingers through hers and tugged her toward a wooden bench surrounded by impeccably designed shrubbery.

"This garden is lovely, but I still like yours better." Her voice was soft and faraway as she took in her surroundings.

"What was going on in there? Did something upset you?" The vulnerable smile she wore tugged at his heart, and he pulled her closer to his side.

"Not sure if I want to talk about it." She sighed as she buried her face into his neck. "I don't want you to go all overprotective big brother on me again."

"Am I that bad?"

"Worse."

He chuckled into her sweet, silky hair and bent to place a featherlight kiss on her temple. "I promise not to go overboard. I just want you to be happy, and sometimes I lose sight of what *you* want."

"I miss my mom." The slight tremor in her voice broke his heart, but he just tightened his hold on her and waited for her to continue. "I wonder how she would've felt, what she would've done as she watched me grow... going to high school prom, graduating from college. She missed it all."

Michael swallowed past the tightness in his throat. "She would've been so proud of you, Adelaide, and she would've been your biggest cheerleader if she saw the amazing, strong and kind woman you are."

"Do you really believe that, Michael?"

"With all my soul." His heart thundered at her use of his full name. He searched her eyes, and saw strength and determination flare in them.

"And if this strong woman tells you that she wants

you more than anything, what will you do about it?"
She lifted her head and pivoted in her seat to face him.
"Will you tap me on my nose and tell me it's past my
bedtime? Or will you kiss me already?"

"You know what I want," he choked out. He needed
to kiss her more than his next breath.

"No, I don't. I don't know what you want. I only
know what I want."

Before he could form a reply, she leaned in and
brushed her soft, parted lips against his. He moaned,
guttural and hungry, and dragged her into his arms.
He'd waited so long for this. So very long. And she
tasted sweeter than he could've ever imagined. Then
her teeth scraped his bottom lip, and there was nothing
sweet about her. She was fire and sin.

With a low groan, he ran the tip of his tongue along
the inside of her parted mouth and coaxed her to open
wide. She acquiesced with a luscious sigh and he
plunged deep into her warmth. His fingers dug into
her long, silky hair, and fisted at the base of her neck
so he could tilt her head and taste her properly.

But it wasn't enough. She'd already clawed off his tie
and had his shirt unbuttoned to his sternum. Her hands
were exploring his chest and making their way down
to his abs. He shivered against her touch.

"Adelaide," he begged. He didn't know whether he
wanted her to stop or continue. It was exquisite torture.

Something tugged at the back of his conscience that
they shouldn't go any further, even as his hands shifted
to her hips and down to the slit on her dress. He growled
when his roaming palm met her hot satiny skin, and
moved upward to the juncture of her thigh.

"Michael, please."

Her breath was hot against his ear, and he hissed when her sharp teeth dug into his lobe, but she promptly soothed it with soft flicks of her tongue. He was losing his mind with every passing second, but his protective instinct kicked in not a moment too soon.

This was Adelaide. She wasn't someone he could paw in the middle of a garden. They were in a secluded spot hidden by dense shrubbery, but they were still in public. How could he have put her at risk like this? Wherever this was going, it had to be an absolute secret to protect Adelaide. No one could find out. Taking a hitching breath, Michael gave her a lingering kiss on her lips before setting her away from him.

"Michael?" Lust-glazed eyes sought his, and he nearly pulled her back into his arms.

"We have to stop, baby." He fisted his hands on his lap. "I'm not going to grope you in the middle of a garden at a fifteen-year-old's birthday ball. If we're doing this, we're doing it right."

"*If* we're doing this?" He was taken aback by her tone. "If you back out after that kiss, you will forever be known as chicken scrap in my book."

"If I don't have you after that kiss, I'll burn to dust from the inside out." Relief and lust battled in his gut. Adelaide was a grown woman, and she wanted him. They couldn't fight the attraction anymore, but it couldn't go beyond that.

It wasn't only about the fashion show and her reputation. They couldn't have a future together. For Adelaide to choose Michael meant for her to oppose her grandmother. Without her grandmother's support, Hansol wouldn't be a part of her future. Choosing him meant giving up her dreams, and that was too big a cost for her to pay. No, this could be only a temporary affair. A man and a woman satiating their needs.

"Do you understand what we're doing?" he asked.

"Well, I'm kind of out of practice, but I think I'll manage." She smirked.

"I want you, Adelaide, but I can't promise you a future." He could never offer her forever, because it would be a forever without a family. Bitterness threatened to choke him. "I could only offer you now."

"I wasn't expecting a marriage proposal, Reynolds." She scoffed dismissively. But was there a tremor in her voice? No. Everything in her demeanor screamed confidence and poise. He had to have imagined it. "I want us to be together, but only until the fashion show, and we have to keep this strictly between us. If Grandmother finds out, she would believe the worst of me. You *are* my business associate for the time being, and having a romantic relationship with you is unprofessional by any standards. I can't disappoint her."

"No one will find out. I know what's at stake, and I won't let that happen." He swallowed the bitter taste in his mouth. All they could have was a two-month fling. Even shorter than he'd hoped. "But while we're together, I want all of you. Exclusively. I have more than a few fantasies to live out before this ends."

Two months. *Only two months.* His head screamed it wasn't enough, but he couldn't offer her a future. He had no right to hold on to her longer than she wanted. And that meant he didn't have a minute to spare. He grabbed her hand and pulled both of them up to their feet.

"Come on," he said, tugging her toward the mansion.

"Wait." She allowed herself to be led by him, but she squeezed his hand until he turned to look at her. "Where are we going?"

"My place." He picked up his pace. He didn't plan on letting her leave before dawn.

"Not a chance." She ground to a halt on the patio where the music spilled out through the open doors.

He blinked rapidly, not comprehending her words. "What?"

"You said you wanted to do this right, remember?" He stared suspiciously at the mischief sparkling in her eyes. "You could make me dinner tomorrow night. I'm not hard to please. A tender, juicy steak will do nicely."

"Of course," he replied automatically, even though his bulging pants signaled his body's protest. He was going to sport wood until he had her. Maybe he could offer to make her some crème brûlée tonight rather than wait for dinner a whole day away.

"Awesome. I'll bring the wine," she said with wide innocent eyes that were belied by her sultry smile.

*Adelaide, you wicked, wicked woman. But you'll be my wicked woman soon.*

# Seven

The next day was full of headaches for Michael. One of his young clients had streaked naked across the famed Melrose streets in broad daylight. He was a good guy, but he took a combination of prescription pills that didn't interact well. Neither his doctor nor his pharmacist had warned him about the potential side effects of the mixture. Michael was relieved his client was feeling better now and that they had a sympathetic reason for his faux pas.

While it had been a frantic day of putting fires out, Michael was grateful for it. If not for the distraction, he wouldn't have lasted until the evening. His lips were blue as he stood lighting the grill after his long, cold shower. He wanted to make sure they made it through dinner before he jumped her.

The caprese salad was chilling in the fridge and the crème brûlée was in the oven. He also had a bottle of Veuve Clicquot on ice for some extra liquid courage. Adelaide said she would be bringing the wine, but he wanted to have backup. His nerves were alit with anticipation and good old-fashioned fear. He was finally going to make love to Adelaide.

Michael left the charcoal to burn in the coal chimney and strolled into his open kitchen. He'd knocked out the wall that separated the kitchen from the dining room to enlarge the space. He lived alone in the eight-bedroom house, but he entertained often so he needed a big kitchen and lounge area. The rest of his home—where he and his parents had once lived as a family—was opulent and cold, but the kitchen was always a warm and welcoming place.

Grabbing a dish towel, he opened the bottle of champagne with a muted pop. He brought out two flutes and filled his up to the top and left the other out waiting for his guest. After gulping down half his glass, he breathed deeply through his nose. The berry and crisp apple notes soothed his raw nerves, and he sipped more leisurely at his drink.

When his cell phone buzzed, he was tempted not to check the text. He didn't want anyone or anything intruding on their evening. Coming to a decision, he pulled out his phone to turn it off, but Adelaide's name caught his eye.

"Hell," he muttered. He had a feeling she wasn't texting him from the front door.

Michael, I had to turn around and go home when I was

ten minutes from your house. Grandmother has summoned me.

Can't she wait until tomorrow?

o__o... Seriously? Why don't you ask her that? Tell her
you have dibs on me tonight.

Michael growled with frustration, and downed the
rest of his champagne before answering.

Come back and have a glass of champagne then go.

You got us champagne?

Yup, and I have crème brûlée in the oven. It'll be ready
in three minutes and I have fresh berries in the fridge
to top it with.

Gob. Stop being a meanie.

*Gob? What the hell is a gob?* he asked himself.

God. I meant God. Stupid voice text.

I don't care. Come.

Aw, poor Michael is sad I'm not coming to play.

Damn right I'm sad.

Well, if it's any consolation, you can come to dinner, too. You're always welcome.

Michael glanced at his watch and made a list of things to put out and turn off before he left so he didn't burn his house down.

I'll be there in forty minutes.

I can't wait.

Neither can I.

He liked it. This sudden freedom to say what he felt. He really liked it. Spurred on by a burst of energy, Michael was in the garage in less than fifteen minutes. He jumped into his restored Mustang; it somehow seemed like the most fitting car for running after a woman. Grinning like an idiot with his heart pummeling his ribs, he liberally interpreted the speed limit and reached the Song residence in less than twenty minutes.

He pushed himself out of the car and grabbed the crème brûlée from his back seat. He couldn't arrive empty-handed. Luckily, he'd made four ramekins of it so there would be enough for Mrs. Song and Adelaide's father.

Michael sprinted up to the front door and rang the bell once, resisting the urge to lean on it.

"That was fast," Adelaide said, smiling warmly as she opened the door.

Without answering, he grasped her hand with his free one and hurried up the staircase.

"Michael," she whispered but followed him with light, soundless footsteps. "What are you doing?"

He tugged her through her bedroom door, pushing her up against it at the same time he closed it with a quiet click. Before she could ask the question in her eyes, he took her mouth in a kiss that had been burning inside him for the last twenty-four hours. He growled when Adelaide opened her mouth in silent invitation, rising on her toes and pressing her body flush against his. He hissed when her hands grabbed his ass, squeezing hard. He jerked helplessly against her touch.

"God, I've been wanting to do that since that night at the club," she confessed with a shy laugh.

He chuckled breathlessly, finding he couldn't formulate a coherent sentence. Instead, he trailed his lips down the side of her neck. Her quiet moan of approval made him so hard it hurt. Then a smart knock sounded at her door, and they jumped apart as though a bucket of ice water had been hurled at them.

"Hey, Adelaide." Colin Song's voice rang in the hallway. "Are you in there?"

"Yeah…yes," she said, grasping Michael's shirt in panic. "What are you doing here?"

"You don't know, either? I was hoping you'd be able to give me a heads-up. I have no idea why *Hal-muh-nee* asked me over." There was a short pause and Michael had the sneaking suspicion that Adelaide's cousin had his ear pressed to her door. "What's going on in there? Why are we talking through a door?"

"This *is* my bedroom and I like to change without an audience." She motioned for Michael to hide in her bathroom. Once he was secure behind the bathroom door, she opened her door. "Why are you hanging around outside my room anyways? You do know the way to the kitchen, don't you?"

"I told you I was hoping for some intel. Besides, your dad's in New York, and I wasn't going to sit at a table with just Grandma Grace presiding. Her soul-piercing gaze would make me pour out all my darkest secrets…"

Their voices grew smaller as they made their way down the stairs. Michael glanced up at his reflection and shook his head. Once again, he had let their kiss get out of hand. All he'd wanted was a minute alone with Adelaide before they joined everyone for dinner. *Damn.* He had to get himself under control. But that was easier said than done when the object of his desire was Adelaide.

He splashed some cold water on his face and tidied his hair. Once he looked presentable, he looked out to the hall to make sure the coast was clear before making his way to the kitchen. He was new to this sneaking-around thing, and he absolutely hated it. But it was the only way he could hold on to Adelaide. When their affair ended in two months, he could go back to being an old family friend. He would play it safe and not get between Adelaide and her grandmother. That way he wouldn't have to let her go completely. He would stay in the good graces of the Song family and still be in Adelaide's life.

He heard the boisterous voice of Colin Song, the family's black sheep. He was the only one who could coax a belly laugh out of the family matriarch. It was good to have him join them for dinner.

"Knock, knock," Michael said, walking into the

small family gathering. "I pestered Adelaide for an invite. It's been a while since I visited, Mrs. Song."

"My granddaughter informed me that you were quite busy assisting with the charity fundraiser. I appreciate all your help, Michael."

"Here." He handed her the carefully packed bag containing the ramekins of crème brûlée. "I brought us dessert."

"They look wonderful. Thank you, my dear."

"I'll put them away for now," Adelaide said, rising from her seat. "It's best served cold."

"Let me help you." They walked farther into the kitchen, past the divider to where the fridge was. Then he whispered in her ear, "I can't believe you hid me in your bathroom."

Her back was turned toward him, but he saw the tips of her ears redden. "I couldn't exactly hide you in my bed, could I?"

"Why not? I could've waited for you to come upstairs tonight like your personal Big Bad Wolf."

"Behave, Reynolds." She glanced over her shoulder and smiled at him.

When they returned to the table and took up their seats, a sneaky grin lit up Colin's face. "I didn't hear the doorbell, Mike. When exactly did you get here?"

*Hell.* The clever bastard was digging. He must've seen his Mustang in the driveway before he came up to Adelaide's room.

*"Hal-muh-nee."* Adelaide spoke over Colin's next words. "My dear cousin and I were wondering why you wanted him here tonight. Other than the pleasure of his company, of course."

"I haven't seen you in so long, Colin." Grace Song's voice softened with emotion. "Your visits are becoming much too rare."

Colin was immediately on his feet and rushed to wrap his arms around his grandmother's shoulders from behind. "I'm so sorry, *Hal-muh-nee.*"

She patted his hand. "I understand why you want to distance yourself from Hansol in public, but that shouldn't keep you from your family, child."

"I know. I'm sorry. I've been very busy getting my production company set up, but things are finally falling into place. I promise I'll visit more often."

"That's better." Mrs. Song smiled, then made a show of shaking his arms off her and they settled into eating.

When dinner was finished, Michael stood up from his seat. "The dessert needs a few final touches. Could you show me where you keep your blowtorch, Adelaide?"

"Sit down, Michael." Mrs. Song said. "Dessert can wait a few more minutes."

"Of course, Mrs. Song." Michael took his seat again, glancing at Adelaide with yearning in his eyes.

She sensed the sheerest tendrils of frustration coming off him and couldn't help but smile when his fingers tangled with hers under the table. But her musings came to an end when her grandmother addressed her.

"I've been receiving reports of your progress on the fashion show. And I am exceedingly pleased with how much you've accomplished."

"Thank you, *Hal-muh-nee.*" She flushed with pride

and surprise at her compliment. "There's still so much left to be done, but I promise not to disappoint you."

"I will, of course, hold you to that promise. And if you convince me that there's a future in the market for a line of sensory-friendly clothing, you would make an ideal lead to launch that design team at Hansol. So your work is just beginning, and I'm watching you with great interest. I expect you to continue to show me your solid work ethic and professionalism through it all."

"The head of the sensory-friendly design team? I don't know what to say." Was this really happening? After two years, she finally had a chance to play a role in Hansol. A major role. Michael squeezed her hand under the table. "Thank you."

"I believe you'll get there, but the thank-you is a little premature. You have much work ahead of you."

"I know, *Hal-muh-nee*," Adelaide replied, her back straightening with resolve. "I'm doing this."

Colin and Grandmother smiled at her with pride and affection. At the lull in the conversation, Michael excused himself and went to the back of the kitchen. Adelaide joined him just as he was setting down the tray of crème brûlée on the counter.

She couldn't help it. She had to touch him. Her hands moved of their own accord and ran down his arm, and he folded her into his arms, resting his cheek on top of her head.

"Congratulations, Adelaide. How are you so amazing? You moved the immovable Grace Song."

"Thank you, Michael. But I'm not there, yet. Like Grandmother said, I still have a long way to go." She drew back to look into his eyes and found them warm and tender. But when her gaze flicked to his lips, then back to his eyes, desire flared to life in them.

"I can't believe you guys left me alone with her," Colin said, making Adelaide and Michael jump apart for the second time that evening. "I thought you just had to torch the tops. What's taking you so long?"

"I'm waiting for Adelaide to remember where the blowtorch is." Michael winked and tousled her hair.

She rolled her eyes at him, but was grateful for his quick thinking. On the other hand, it bothered her how composed he seemed when her heart was racing like a roadrunner.

Besides, Colin wasn't fooled for a second. Adelaide ignored him and went to open a few cupboards, pretending to search for something. Her cousin coughed into his fist to cover what sounded like a snort. Without reacting to his teasing, she finally opened the drawer holding the blowtorch, and handed it to Michael. If anyone other than Colin knew about her and Michael, she'd be in a panic, but her cousin wasn't under the crazy overprotective spell everyone else in her family seemed to be under.

Michael made quick work of sprinkling some sugar over the cooled cream, and caramelized the tops into a crunchy, bittersweet layer. "Let's go eat before Mrs. Song comes marching in here next."

The three of them returned to the dining table to find Grandmother nodding off. Adelaide's heart constricted at the vulnerable sight. *Hal-muh-nee* was getting older and more fragile every year. The thought of losing her terrified Adelaide so much she couldn't breathe for a second.

Michael squeezed her shoulder as though he sensed her panic. "You should help her to her room."

"Yeah." Adelaide gently placed her hand over her arm. "*Hal-muh-nee*, let me take you to your room. It's late."

"I'll help you," Colin said, coming to hold their grandmother's other arm.

As they turned to head out into the hallway, Michael caught Adelaide's eyes and mouthed, *See you soon.* Her body protested at losing the one thing that could satisfy its hunger, but she turned her thoughts to taking care of Grandmother. *See you.*

Colin waited outside while Adelaide helped her change into her pajamas, and set out her firm quilt and pillow on the floor. Once Grandmother was settled, she placed a soft blanket over her. "Good night. I love you."

"I know, *Yoon-ah.*"

Adelaide froze with her hand on the door, startled by her grandmother's affectionate words. But when she turned around, her grandmother was already sound asleep, her blanket rising and falling with her soft, steady breathing.

Colin stood outside the door, staring forlornly at his feet.

"Hey, cuz," she whispered.

"How is she?"

"She's just a little tired. She fell asleep as soon as her head hit the pillow." Adelaide drew in a deep breath. "She misses you, though."

"I'll come visit her more often. CS Productions has been taking up all my time lately." He sighed and raked his fingers through his hair. "That's a lame excuse. I just don't want to disappoint her like Father did."

"You're not your father. Uncle chose his own path. Like I've said a million times, it's not Hansol and the Song name that made him who he was. You could be part of Hansol and be ten times the man he is."

"Which wouldn't be a difficult feat since he never lifted a finger to fend for himself. The man only knew how to take." Colin's smile was blinding in its sorrow. "I don't need you to worry about me, though. I can take care of myself."

"Oh, yeah. Sure, you can."

She rolled her eyes to cover the tears stinging them, because Colin never knew any other way. He'd always taken care of himself. On his own. Adelaide wished Colin had someone who could take care of him for once. Well, someone he would let take care of him.

Sensing her melancholy, he bumped her shoulder as they walked side by side to the front door. She bumped him back.

"Never forget I've got your back," she said with quiet conviction.

"Ditto." He swung his arm around her shoulder and kissed her temple, a million unsaid words traveling between them.

# Eight

Adelaide stepped out of the shower after a few minutes, too tired to linger. Besides, a cold shower wasn't exactly relaxing. She tugged on her cami-and-shorts set and climbed into bed, missing Michael.

Listless and frustrated, she tossed and turned in her bed and didn't hear the knocking at her window at first. When she finally heard, she jumped out of bed and peeked out. A big, hulking figure stood outside in the shadows and she had to stifle a scream behind her hand. Then a man stepped into the light, his hands held out in front of him in surrender.

"Michael?" She quickly unlocked her French doors and pulled him inside unceremoniously. "What are you doing out there? You almost gave me a heart attack."

"There's no way I'm leaving without holding you tonight."

His growly voice got her hot and bothered, but the thought of making love with him with her grandmother downstairs was deeply disturbing.

"Tonight? Here? But…we can't. Grandma's right downstairs—"

His dark chuckle sent shivers down her spine. "I said I wanted to hold you. I never said anything about… other activities."

Adelaide was grateful her moonlit room probably hid her blush from him. "So you just want to hold me?"

"Yes, I want to hold you." He stepped closer and wrapped her waist with his hands. "When I make love to you the first time, you're going to be screaming my name. We can't have you doing that here. Can we?"

Not trusting herself to speak, Adelaide just shook her head.

"I'm glad we're on the same page now."

With a wolfish grin, Michael unbuttoned his shirt and shrugged out of it. She couldn't stop the gasp that escaped her lips at the sight of his bare torso. He was so perfect. She bit her lip, dying to run her hands over his sculpted chest and abs.

She might have whimpered a little when he tugged off his belt and unzipped his pants. "Are you sure we're not doing any…other activities?"

He stepped out of the pants that had pooled at his feet, and pushed off his shoes and socks. "I didn't say we weren't doing *any* activities."

Michael strode toward her with determination, and Adelaide retreated until she backed into her bed. Her legs couldn't hold her up a second longer, so she sank down on the edge of the mattress. When his knee settled beside her hip, she scooted back until she was pressed up against her headboard. He crawled to her and tugged her legs until she lay flat on her back. She let out a nervous squeak.

"Hush," he said against the sensitive skin of her neck, and kissed his way up to her jaws. "Relax. It's just me."

"Just you?" she choked out. "Right. And that makes this the most normal thing ever? You near naked in my bed doing delicious things to me. Sure, you're just good ol' Mike."

He bit her earlobe hard enough for her to suck in a startled breath. "Don't call me that."

"What? Mike?"

He grunted as he trailed kisses to the other side of her neck, and a tremulous smile touched the corner of her mouth. He knew he was *her* Michael. And he wanted to be hers.

"That's right. You're not just Mike, are you?" She boldly slid her hands down his back and thrilled when his muscles jumped and clenched beneath her touch. "You're my Michael. And you want me so badly you're nearly losing your mind. Isn't that right, *Michael*?"

"God, yes," he groaned.

His mouth finally crushed into hers and the desperation of the kiss took her breath and sense away. All that it left behind was hunger. His hard thigh slid between her legs and put delicious pressure on her.

"Yes," she echoed.

"You feel like silk against me. Very cold silk."

She slid her hands inside his boxer shorts and

squeezed his round, taut behind, and he hissed into her ear.

"It's actually a little odd how cold you are." He lifted his head to study her face. "Your hands are freezing."

*Oh, hell.*

"Adelaide?" A teasing tone entered Michael's voice and his hand roamed up and down the length of her arm. "Why is your skin so freezing cold?"

"I…uh…shut up." She wrapped her arms around him and buried her face in his neck so he couldn't look at her.

"Your hair is damp. Did you take a shower?" he asked, running his fingers through her hair.

"Yes."

"Was it a cold shower?"

"Yes."

"Why, Adelaide? Tell me."

"Because I wanted you so much it hurt." She drew her face back from his neck and met his searching gaze. "But the shower wasn't enough to stop me from aching for you. If you'd knocked on the veranda door five minutes later, I would've been touching myself, thinking of you."

"God, Adelaide. You're going to kill me."

This time when his lips crushed into hers, it wasn't just desperation but a soul-wrenching yearning that awakened an echoing hunger inside her. She flipped their positions and straddled him. He dragged in a shuddering breath, then flipped them to their sides and tucked her face against his chest.

"What are you doing?" Adelaide asked, bewildered and frustrated as hell.

"We've done as many 'other things' as I can humanly handle for tonight." He draped his arm over his eyes.

"You're right. My grandmother's right downstairs, even though she's out cold for the night."

"Go to sleep. I'll hold you until you fall asleep."

"Okay."

She wrapped her arm around his naked waist and snuggled against him, her heartbeat slowing to a brisk but steady tempo. There was no way her pulse could return to normal with Michael near naked beside her. It felt like a dream, yet more searingly real than any other moment in her life.

"Good night," she said with a content sigh, and kissed his cheek and settled her head on his muscular chest. God, she loved his pecs—broad enough to cradle the ocean in his arms. "Will I see you tomorrow?"

"Hell, yes." His arms tightened around her. "You won't be able to get out of our dinner date again."

She laughed softly, delighted by the hint of possessiveness in his voice. She wanted him crazy for her. "Don't forget. I like my steak rare, my champagne dry and my dessert…decadent."

"You can count on me to deliver, sweetheart," he said in a low voice that made her toes curl.

With frissons of sweet anticipation running down her back, Adelaide let her exhausted body drift off to sleep.

When he got home, Michael stripped out of his clothes and climbed into bed. He could still taste her on his lips and remembered the smooth coolness of her skin against his hands. *Damn.* The thought of her taking a cold shower because she burned for him drove him insane and turned him rock hard in an instant.

He reached for himself and squeezed, groaning roughly. Having kissed her and held her nearly naked body, he couldn't stop wanting to bury himself deep inside her hot, wet core. He pumped his hand once, and hissed through his teeth. But he wasn't about to spend himself on a towel when he only had a day to wait for the real thing. It was his turn for a cold shower. His second of the day.

Michael stood under the cold water until his teeth chattered, but it barely took the edge off his wild desire for Adelaide. *Tomorrow. I'll have you tomorrow.*

The next morning dawned with the sun streaming through the gap in his curtains and the melodic song of cheerful birds outside. Michael gritted his teeth and pulled his pillow over his head. The monstrous morning wood greeting him after barely two hours of sleep made him cranky and beyond frustrated.

Maybe he should cancel his back-to-back client meetings, go kidnap Adelaide from her studio and bring her home like a caveman. Because he certainly felt like one at the moment.

He flung away the covers, headed straight for the shower and ran the water full blast on its coldest setting. He swore as he stepped under the punishing stream and methodically went through each issue he had to address in his meetings. *Do not—EVER—drink and drive. You can freaking afford to pay for a cab. Don't get high and go out on a burger binge. People will take pictures of you at your sloppiest and post it.* He shook his head at the idiotic messes his clients made. It was frustrating as hell, but thinking about it had the desired effect of killing his more amorous feelings.

Once he was ready, he stepped out of his house dressed in his dark gray suit and sea-blue tie. Adelaide had gotten him the tie a couple birthdays ago. It was embroidered with little silver sharks with menacing grins. It suited his mood—lack of sleep and sexual frustration made him feel snappy—and it made him feel closer to Adelaide.

"Good morning, Mr. Reynolds," the receptionist greeted him with a bright smile.

"Trisha," he said with a stiff nod, and quickly made his way to his office. He didn't want to bite anyone's head off in his sullen mood.

The maintenance calls were kept short and sweet whereas the troubleshooting calls took many patience-testing minutes. But either way, the day stretched on like saltwater taffy, and his hair stood on its ends from running his hands through it repeatedly. The last meeting ran over and he didn't leave his office until past eight.

As he drove out of the parking structure, heart pumping at the thought of finally seeing Adelaide, his phone screen alerted him to an incoming call.

"Did you miss me?" Michael said, picking up the call.

"Like crazy," Garrett deadpanned.

Michael laughed, happy to hear from his best friend. "How's the CEO gig? The company still standing?"

"Screw you, Reynolds. It's doing better than ever

and you know it. Your stock in the company must be making you a pretty penny these days."

"Yeah, I'm rolling in dough. How are the East Coast Song ladies doing?"

"You won't believe it. Sophie talks in phrases now. Nonstop. Natalie and I can't believe how much she has to say." He was right. Michael couldn't believe the baby girl Garrett and his wife adopted was already a toddler. "Too bad I can't understand half of it. Natalie seems to know exactly what she's saying, though." Garrett's words flew out in a hurry, and he cleared his throat loudly.

"Are you nervous about something, Song? What's going on?"

"Natalie's pregnant." Garrett sounded elated and mildly panicked.

"Congratulations! Are Natalie and the baby doing well?"

"Yeah. We just had our first ultrasound, and the baby's heartbeat sounded like a chugging train. It was amazing. Truly amazing. Sophie nicknamed the baby Peanut because of the ultrasound image."

"I'm so happy for you. You'll do great. You're already an amazing father."

Michael pulled his car over, feeling overwhelmed. The news of his best friend and his wife having a child together filled him with joy and pride, but a shadow of pitiful envy tainted his happiness. Guilt stabbed at his gut. Garrett was his closest friend. *How can I be anything but happy for him?*

"Thanks, Michael. That means a lot to me."

"It's the truth. Congratulations, Garrett."

He raked both hands through his hair once they ended the call. He was having difficulty dragging in a full breath. *What the hell is wrong with me?* He thought he'd gotten rid of his longing for a child of his own, but the devastation and shame of his infertility seemed to have clung stubbornly to the dark recesses of his mind.

He was done feeling sorry for himself. Natalie was pregnant, and it was the best damn news he'd gotten in ages. It was also a timely reminder why he couldn't have anything long-term with Adelaide. She had grown up lonely, and he was certain she wanted children someday. Children he couldn't give her.

When he made love to Adelaide, he had to keep a part of himself locked away. He couldn't fall for her. He couldn't stray from his decision not to hold on to her. It would just be for a short while. A couple months to store up on a lifetime of memories. He deserved that much. *Didn't he?*

A few minutes later, he walked into Adelaide's studio with his hair tousled, stubble on his jaw, tie askew and dark circles under his eyes. It was late, and he was surprised to find Mona, the student who'd taken a hiatus to raise her kids, Chris, and Cindy still hard at work.

Adelaide soon came into view and everything about her was perfect. She was wearing a soft pink sleeveless top, and black ankle pants that complemented her figure and coloring. Her head was bent over the desk with her long hair tucked behind her ears, and her fuchsia-stained bottom lip caught between her teeth. *God, she's sexy as sin.*

"Oh." She was so immersed in her sketch that it took her a few minutes to notice him standing by her desk.

She blinked at him as though he'd manifested from thin air. "When did you get here?"

"Five minutes ago." He smiled at the pure pleasure of hearing her beautiful voice. "I didn't want to interrupt your work."

She lifted her hand as though to touch his arm, but quickly withdrew it. Not only had they promised to keep their affair discreet, but any kind of touching in front of her design team would be unprofessional. Instead, they stood two feet apart, devouring each other with their eyes. Adelaide looked away first, clearing her throat. He enjoyed how much his proximity affected her, and a cocky grin spread across his face. She fanned the top of her shirt before throwing up her hands. Her gestures seemed to say, *Fine. I want you. You win.*

"*Moving on.* I had this idea about using a secret panel to make slacks that are well-fitted yet comfortable around the waist and zipper area." As she spoke, excitement crept into her voice. "I got the idea while shopping for Natalie's maternity clothes earlier. Garrett told you, right?"

"I thought they just found out she was pregnant," he said. "Why would she need maternity clothes already?"

"Who said anything about her needing them? And that's not the point." She waved her hand impatiently, brushing off his question like an annoying fly. "The überflexible material they use for maternity clothes stretches an incredible amount then returns to its original form without pressing too tightly against your skin or hanging loose."

"So you want to make stretchy slacks? How are they

different from, say, jeggings? Or children's pants with elastics in the back."

"First of all, jeggings? Seriously? People can't wear tight, stretchy leggings to a traditional work space. At least, not in good taste. Second, having the elastic in the back of the pants will increase discomfort. The elasticized area will be ridged, crinkled and scratchy." She wrinkled her nose at him. "What I can do is create slacks from conventional materials but add a small secret panel behind the zippered front, so you can easily pull them on like sweats, but the waist conforms to the exact size you want, so nothing digs into your skin. Or hangs too loose, which would require a belt, and that probably feels like torture to people with sensory-processing difficulties. Nobody thinks belts are comfortable."

"Breathe, Adelaide. I hear you. I can't picture exactly how it'll work, but the idea sounds brilliant."

"But I'm going to need some input from the design team tomorrow. I should have some potential designs to discuss by then," she mumbled, turning toward her desk.

"You work. I'll go pick up dinner," he said. Her head bobbed up and down, signaling her absentminded consent. So much for a romantic dinner at his place. He smiled wistfully as he left her side. "Would you three like some dinner? I could pick some up for you," he said to the rest of the design team as he passed them.

"We'll take a rain check on that. We're leaving in a few minutes to grab chili cheeseburgers at Tommy's." Cindy spoke up for all of them. "But thanks for asking."

"No problem. Have fun," Michael said, and left the studio.

Even when she was little, if Adelaide had a task to complete, she would work nonstop until she finished. He needed some finger food that he could feed her while she sketched. Sushi or *gimbap*? They had sushi a few days ago, and he couldn't find good *gimbap* at this time of night. He got it. Bite-size dumplings would do the job.

The closest dumpling restaurant was in Chinatown, which was about twenty minutes away. He wouldn't get back until past ten o'clock, but Adelaide wouldn't even notice she was hungry. She'd be ravenous once she smelled the food, though.

Michael got in his car and headed toward LA's Chinatown. He barely got there before the last call for orders and ordered half the menu. He made good time back to Hansol, his growling stomach hurrying him along. The food smelled amazing.

As he expected, Adelaide sat exactly where he'd left her with balls of crumpled paper overflowing from her trash can. She'd been working hard, but she probably wasn't happy with her progress.

"Just don't go hangry on me," he said, plopping down the box of food on the shared table in the middle of the room. "Would you like to take a break for a few minutes and eat at the table, or do you want me to feed you?"

She glanced up and frowned, then looked back down.

Michael laughed, shaking his head. She was lost in her world, and he didn't want to disrupt her creative process. Besides, he was looking forward to feeding her. It was nearly ten o'clock so they had the studio to themselves. Still he peeked out to the hallway to make sure no one was around. Feeding her dumplings while she sketched was innocuous enough, but he didn't want to risk being seen.

"Open wide." He pushed aside the dirty thoughts invading his brain, and popped a shrimp-and-chives dumpling in her waiting mouth.

"Mmm." Finally. A semiverbal response.

Next he fed her a pork-and-shrimp shumai, and ate one himself.

"Again," she said. He obligingly popped in another shumai. Next time, he would have to get two orders of it.

By the time they finished dinner, Adelaide had a finished sketch that she didn't crumple up.

"See. You should never work on an empty stomach," he said, gesturing to her design.

"I guess you're right." She looked up from the sketch and smiled widely at him. "This is pretty good."

He reached out and cupped her cheek, and she leaned into his hand. "You're never just pretty good. You're exceptional."

"I think you're a little biased," she said, blushing a lovely pink.

Unable to stop himself, he kissed her lightly on the lips. She moved to deepen the kiss, but he moved back after another soft brush of his lips. "You still have work to do. I don't want to distract you. If you kiss me like you mean it, I might carry you out of here."

She pretended to pout, shy pleasure in her expression. "You're no fun, Reynolds."

He laughed and dropped a kiss on the tip of her nose.

"I'll be at that desk over there minding my own business."

"It's late. You should go home and rest." She grabbed his hand and threaded her fingers through his. "You don't need to stay."

He squeezed her hand, which was saying the opposite of her words. "I want to keep you company, and make sure you don't spend the whole night here."

"I'm too old to pull an all-nighter, but I guess you can stay. You obviously want to ogle me some more."

"Like I said, I'll be at that desk over there undressing you with my eyes," he said in a low voice. Adelaide leaned into him as though mesmerized, and he kissed her sweet lips one last time. "Get to work, Song."

Michael turned on his tablet and began his everyday recon for bad publicity affecting his clients. It was a good day without any publicity nightmares, but recon was the most mundane part of his job. When he was done, he pinched the bridge of his nose and closed his dry eyes tight. A glance at his watch told him it was close to two, and Adelaide was still stooped over her sketchbook.

"How's it going?" he asked, gently massaging her stiff shoulders.

She smothered a yawn behind her hand before relaxing into the massage. "I finished two and just started the third design."

"It's two in the morning. Maybe you can finish the third one after a few hours of sleep. You need to be able to function tomorrow. I'll drive you home, so you could sleep in the car."

"I don't want to wake up Grandmother. She's a

light sleeper." She smiled sweetly. "Can we go to your place?"

"Yes."

He couldn't say no when she wanted to be with him, but she needed rest. He wouldn't touch her tonight. At least, he would try hard not to touch her. Very hard.

# Nine

Adelaide must've fallen asleep in the car. She was jostled awake when Michael lifted her out of the passenger seat and carried her to his house. Once they were inside, he gently lowered her feet to the floor and set her away from him. He stared at his shoes for a second as though he was unsure about what to do.

"I'll show you to the…" He glanced at her, then looked away.

Why the awkwardness? She frowned. They were finally alone, and she wanted him. Adelaide was barely awake and making words was hard, so she linked her fingers through his and led him up the stairs. She'd only seen the room he used as a boy, but figured he would have a bed and a bathroom in the master bedroom. He indeed had an en suite bathroom, but when she led him toward it Michael halted before the threshold.

"What are you doing?" His husky voice spread warmth across her skin.

"I'm taking you into the shower with me so I can get you wet and naked," she said, holding his gaze.

"I can't. We can't. You need to rest. I can't become a distraction to your work."

"But I need your brand of distraction right now. All work and no play makes me a very frustrated girl. I have needs and sleep isn't on the top of my list right this moment." She drew closer to him, grabbing a fistful of his shirt, and allowed her voice to vibrate with her desire. "Listen, I'm going to scream and kick something if I don't have you tonight."

He sucked in a sharp breath, and his eyes lit with a smoldering fire. But he continued to resist. "Adelaide, your work is so important to you—"

"Let me set some ground rules for this relationship. I get to have you whenever I want, wherever I want, and I want to have you right here tonight. Got it?"

She saw the shift in him immediately. The concerned groove between his eyebrows smoothed out and his lips tilted into a wolfish grin. The predatory air around him made her take a small step back. His grin turning cocky, he stalked her step by step until she was backed up against the glass shower door. Her breaths were already coming faster.

*God, I'm so turned-on.*

"So you want to get me wet and naked?"

She nodded emphatically. She was past the point of coherent speech.

"Do you want to watch me undress?"

"Yes," she managed to rasp.

"How badly?" Now he was just teasing. She was so going to get him back for that.

"Badly. Please."

He removed his watch with a deliberate movement and set it on the counter. Then he took his time releasing his cuff links and she got a glimpse of his wrist. It was so sexy. She was in so much trouble if she got hot over a flash of wrist. Then, with dexterous fingers, he undid his shirt buttons one by one, showing more and more tantalizing skin. When he shifted his shoulders and let the shirt drop to the floor, Adelaide gasped and bit her lip hard.

Her hands rose of their own accord and reached for his sculpted abs.

"Tsk, tsk," he said, taking a step back. "I didn't say you could touch me...yet."

"What?" She actually stomped her foot like a bratty first-grader. But she was desperate. Her mind commanded her to touch, kiss and lick every inch of his body. *Now.*

"You can watch, but you can't touch until I tell you to. Understood?" he said in a voice that demanded complete obedience.

"But—"

"Understood?" he repeated, his hands going to the buckle of his belt. "Or should I stop right now?"

"No, don't stop. I understand. I do. Okay?"

His smile turning wicked, he unbuckled his belt and slowly tugged it off. When he unzipped his pants, she whimpered like an eager puppy. She couldn't feel embarrassment. He was driving her out of her mind.

When he revealed the rest of himself, and kicked away his pants and boxer briefs, Adelaide stood mesmerized. Her dreams fell far short of reality, and the reality stole her breath.

"Do I meet your approval?" The arrogant rise of his eyebrow told her he already knew her answer.

"Oh, I don't know." She grinned when his knowing smirk faltered. "I have to determine whether we're a good…fit."

"Oh, I'm sure we'll fit perfectly," he purred as he lifted her shirt, his fingers skimming the sensitive skin of her sides. The hair on her arms rose to attention, and a shiver trilled down her spine as she raised her arms over her head.

He released the clasp of her bra with unsteady fingers. His calm arrogance was falling apart as he uncovered more of her body. The sense of power released her from her momentary timidity.

"Well, then. Prove it," she said, gently pushing aside his fumbling hands from the button of her pants.

She quickly undid the button and zipper herself, and wiggled out of her pants. Her bravado failed her when it came to her panties. So she stood tall in front of him wearing a scrap of lace.

"My God, Adelaide." He reached out and touched her shoulders, then moved them down her arms. He got down on his knees and peeled her panties off, and said almost reverently, "You're so perfect."

Before her shyness surfaced again, she stepped closer to him and turned the shower on. Michael slowly came to his feet, his hands traveling up her torso, then cupping her heavy, sensitive breasts. She gasped at the lovely sensation of his touch, both rough and gentle.

When the shower filled with steam, he wrapped his hands around her waist and lifted her into the stall. She moved under the water stream to give him room to join her. He stepped into the shower, and his tall, broad body filled the roomy space, turning it into their own cozy cocoon.

"Your turn to get wet." Licking her lips with anticipation, she grasped his shoulders and spun them in a circle so he stood under the water. Drops of water trailed down his toned torso and below. *Gulp.* He looked intimidatingly handsome.

He blocked the direct stream of the shower with his wide back and pulled her into his arms. She pressed against him with a happy sigh and tilted her face up for a kiss. Michael cupped her cheek and rained down featherlight kisses on her face, taking his sweet time before reaching her mouth.

He pressed a lingering kiss on one corner of her lips, then another. She was too frustrated to wait for him to kiss her properly. When he brushed his lips fully against hers, she dug her fingers into his soaking hair and pulled his face down. She sucked his bottom lip into her mouth, but when he didn't open his mouth right away, she bit down, not so gently. He jerked a little and hissed, but didn't move away.

She took advantage of his slackened mouth and drove her tongue inside. A shudder ran through him, and the hand cupping her face moved to her hair and fisted in it. He tilted her face as he plunged his tongue into her mouth, devouring her like a man starved. As his reward for complying with her wishes, Adelaide sucked his bottom lip into her mouth again and laved the spot she had bitten with her tongue, soothing away any lingering pain.

"God," he groaned, his chest rumbling beneath her roaming hands. "I want you so much."

"Then take me, Michael."

His head dipped to kiss her along her jaw, to her collarbone and down to the curves of her breasts. He dropped soft, openmouthed kisses on the sides, getting tantalizingly close to her hard peaks. She arched her back and pushed herself to him when his mouth finally closed over one. She whimpered as her hips moved against his thighs, seeking desperately for friction.

"Ride me." He nudged her legs open with his knee and nestled his thigh between her legs.

And she did. Michael kissed her with raw, feral hunger, and his hands moved possessively over her body as though he needed to touch her everywhere at once. She was so close. He dropped to his knees and spread her legs farther apart.

"Not like this…" She was so close, she couldn't even protest properly. She didn't want to come like this. By herself. She wanted him to come with her, buried inside her. "I…ah…"

He licked her sensitive center like she was an ice-cream cone, laving away at her and scraping his teeth ever so lightly over her. She was moaning and thrashing her head against the shower wall. *Hell.* It was sweet, sweet torture, pleasure intermingling with a need that felt almost painful. Then he sucked her fully into his mouth.

"Michael!" she cried out. Her orgasm slammed into her so hard that her knees buckled. She would've slid down to the ground if it wasn't for Michael holding her up by her hips.

When he stood back up and took in her flushed face, he grinned broadly. "I told you you'd scream my name."

"Uh-huh." That was all she could manage because she was busy gasping for air.

He raised his eyebrow and twisted around to shut off the water. He stepped out of the shower first and quickly dried off. Then he reached for her and gently dried her hair before wrapping her in a towel and lifting her into his arms.

A very naked, very aroused Michael eased her onto the bed, then had the gall to walk away from her.

"Hey," she said, pushing herself onto her elbows. "Where do you think you're going?"

"Condom," he replied from the bathroom.

*Good.* Adelaide discarded her towel and got up on her knees, propping her fists on her waist. She was about to rock his world. When he caught a glimpse of her naked superhero pose, his mouth dropped open and his eyes glazed over.

Taking advantage of his momentary awe, she slid her palms up from her naval to cup her breasts. "Are you ready for me?"

"God, Adelaide."

He quickly closed the distance between them, then crushed her against him as he kissed her with bruising intensity, matching the pulsing desire inside her. With swiftness that made her catch her breath, he laid her on her back and covered her body with his.

*This.*

The pressure of his naked body against hers nearly sent her over the edge. She hungrily scraped her fingers over his muscular back and moved lower to grab his rounded buttocks. When he made a sound like an animal's growl, she wanted to laugh with delight, power and freedom. Then he took the tip of her aching breast into his mouth and any urge to laugh evaporated.

"Michael," she moaned in a voice she hardly recognized as her own. This was Michael. *Her* Michael. And he was making love to her like there was nothing on this planet that he wanted more than her.

His teeth scraped her hard nipple and her back arched off the bed. He pushed her down with his hips and continued his unbearably hot ministrations. She was panting and writhing beneath him, silently begging him for release.

When he didn't relent, she begged in earnest. "Please. Now."

With a grunt, he delved his fingers into her swollen, wet folds and cursed under his breath. "God, you're soaking wet. You're ready for me."

"Yes. Yes, please."

His hot, heavy body shifted off her, and he ripped the package with his teeth. He held himself in one hand and rolled the condom on. It was one of the sexiest sights she'd ever seen. Then he was back on her, the fire in his eyes making her shiver with anticipation. He spread her legs with his knee and positioned himself at her entry.

"Are you sure?" He brushed off her hair from her forehead. "Are you absolutely sure you want me?"

"So much it hurts." Her voice cracked, and she let the vulnerability of her admission shine freely in her eyes. "Now take me already."

He pushed into her and they moaned in unison, and inch by inch he rocked himself deeper until he was buried to the hilt inside her.

"Adelaide. Adelaide."

Breathing her name like a chant, Michael drove them to a tempo that made her wild. She met him push for push, planting her feet on the bed to take him deeper. Then an aching tightness began gathering between her thighs. Seeing that she was close, he tilted her hips up and pumped into her harder and faster. And the waves built higher and higher until her vision went white with an orgasm so deep and strong that tears filled her eyes.

"Michael."

She held tight to him, letting herself get lost in the sensations. Before she fully came down from her orgasm, Michael rode her with fast, erratic movements until he yelled out her name and reached his own release.

He hovered over her, supporting the bulk of his weight on the arms pressed next to her head. But he was trembling, and he slowly eased himself out of her and collapsed to his side, dragging her over with him.

Michael gazed at her with such tenderness that a lump formed in her throat. Tightening his hold on her, he feathered kisses on her head, nose, temple and cheeks, and Adelaide felt absolutely cherished.

"Can we do it again?" she asked.

He chuckled and his chest rumbled wonderfully under her hand. "I'm not a twenty-year-old. Give me a couple hours."

"Wow. You can go again in a couple hours? Okay. I'm game."

"Are you, baby? You make me crazy. Do you know that?"

"I do?"

"Yes. I want you so much I can't see straight."

"Well, we can't have that. I prescribe another round of hot, sweaty sex in two hours." She yawned into her hand. "That'll give us plenty of time to nap."

"Go to sleep, and I'll wake you up in a couple hours." His sexy grin made her stomach flutter with reawakening lust. Still, she closed her eyes. She'd just had the best sex of her life, but she had work to do. After more sex with Michael.

Concerned for her exhaustion and workload, Michael had decided not to seduce her tonight. But that wasn't what Adelaide had in mind. He had gone back to his old habit of being overprotective of her, like she was a young girl who needed his help.

That was where he was wrong. She was a strong woman who knew her own mind. Once she put her foot down and made her desires crystal clear, he didn't have a leg to stand on. Besides, he couldn't say no to her. The willpower to hold himself back was depleted.

He drifted off to exhausted sleep as soon as Adelaide's breathing evened out in her slumber. He'd kept a firm hold on her to remind himself she was his—just for a little while. Still, it was a heady feeling, and even in his sleep he felt overwhelmed by the joy and excitement flowing through him.

Sometime later he woke up to a still-dark room with Adelaide's body pressed against his, her toned, shapely leg thrown over him. He smiled, remembering his promise before he fell asleep, and began drawing slow circles on her back.

She stirred in his arms, then sighed and burrowed deeper into his chest. She was so adorable. With a low chuckle, he pressed a firm kiss on her shoulder, and her eyes fluttered open, then widened.

"Good morning," he said lazily, even though dawn was a while away.

"Good morning," she replied then hid a yawn behind her hand.

He was tempted to let her go back to sleep, but she needed to finish her design. The best thing he could do for her was to help her wake up. So he trailed kisses up her shoulder to the sensitive skin of her neck. She wasn't yawning anymore.

Michael grinned and teased her with featherlight kisses all over her face except for her lips. She began squirming against him, which made him too turned-on to play, and he crushed his mouth on hers, open and hungry.

Their first time hadn't been a fluke. Their desire erupted between them like a force of nature, and they consumed each other as though their survival depended on it. When she came apart in his arms, he followed right after her, and they came down together, panting and sweaty.

"Are you awake now?" he asked, his chest rising and falling like he'd sprinted through downtown.

"Mmm-hmm," she hummed through her nose. She sounded satiated and drowsy.

"Oh, no, you don't." He slapped her shapely behind.

"Ow," she grumbled, trying to hide her grin. She liked that, did she? He choked back his groan.

"You go take a shower. I'll make the coffee," he said firmly, giving her a light push toward the bathroom.

He walked into the kitchen naked, not bothering to tug on clothes over his sweat-slicked body. In a few minutes, he started back toward his room with two steaming mugs of coffee in his hands. But Adelaide strode into the kitchen before he could take more than a couple steps. She was scrubbed clean of makeup and dressed in the same clothes she'd worn the day before. He wanted her so much.

"Are you kidding me, Reynolds?" She threw her hands up. "You're serving me coffee naked? I thought you wanted me to concentrate on my project?"

"Don't go getting any ideas. I can't put my clothes on until I shower." Grinning from ear to ear, Michael gave her coffee and a fleeting kiss. "Here, drink your coffee and get to work. My office is down the hall."

"You're such a tease."

Laughing hard enough to make his coffee slosh in the mug, he made his way to the bathroom. He was still smiling when he stepped out of the shower. He hadn't felt so carefree and lighthearted in a long time. Adelaide had freed something inside him. Something he'd thought was permanently lost. Happiness. She made him happy like nothing else could.

When he peeked into his office an hour later, Adelaide was engrossed in her sketch. He hated to disturb her, but he had to leave for work.

"How's it going, baby?" And because he couldn't help it, he kissed her full, pink lips.

"Like it's on fire," she replied when he pulled back. "I'm so excited about these designs."

"You should be. Your idea sounds phenomenal." He deliberately took a step away from her. "I'm going to leave you to it. You could stay as long as you like."

"What? You're leaving?" There was a note of hurt in her voice. But he had to keep his promise to her. He had to keep their relationship a secret, because no matter how right it felt, it would come to an end.

"We can't both be late to work, and I shouldn't be seen dropping you off at Hansol. We have a good cover to be seen together, but we shouldn't push our luck. Sorry I can't give you a ride back," he said, cupping her soft cheek. A soft cloud of melancholy settled over him at the thought of leaving her.

"Don't be silly. I'll call for a car." She leaned into his hand.

"What time will you be here tonight?" He drew her closer.

"As soon as I can wrap up work?"

"I still owe you dinner."

"That's right." A lovely smile curved her lips. "One kiss goodbye?"

"God, yes."

She stood on her tiptoes and planted her lips against his. Her kiss was sweet and full of promise, and brimming with suppressed desire. He responded in kind, because neither of them would have the strength to pull away if they kissed like they wanted to.

# Ten

Adelaide was running on coffee and adrenaline by the time she got the whole team together. A few of the designers had class till the late afternoon, so it was past six when she held the meeting to go over her latest sketches.

"Any thoughts? Suggestions? Constructive criticism?" she asked, her palms sweating.

Her team was humming with excitement while Adelaide gave her quick presentation, but they turned still and silent the moment she finished. It was a few nerve-racking seconds before they all burst out talking at once.

"The pants will fit different body shapes and in-between sizes perfectly and comfortably."

"My brother would love this," she heard Chris say in the clamor.

"This might give people on the spectrum clothing choices that's affordable and comfortable."

"You guys," Adelaide interrupted, laughter rippling through her. "Hang on a moment. I appreciate your enthusiasm, but so far it's only an idea. There are a lot of things to figure out before we can turn this idea into a reality."

"I don't see something as abstract as an amorphous idea floating around. I see kindling already starting to smoke," Cindy chimed in, bouncing on her feet. "Soon we'll have a bonfire. This is amazing!"

"And remember this isn't the only idea we're working with. You guys have been coming up with innovative ways to dispel the belief that looking sharp and being comfortable are mutually exclusive." Adelaide made eye contact with each of her talented team members. "*You* are doing this."

An enthusiastic burst of cheers rang out in the studio. Adelaide decided to take the opportunity to broach the subject of models. She wanted this fashion show and her future sensory-friendly clothing line to be part of society's attempt to accept differences rather than ostracize and judge those who weren't "normal." *Who defines "normal" anyway?* A world of "normal" people lined up like sardines in a giant can was the stuff of dark, dystopian novels.

"Everyone, can I get your attention again?" The room quieted in an instant. The level of respect this group gave her truly humbled her. "Our fashion show is about celebrating differences, right? So I think our models should also reflect those differences."

"You mean you want to use models with real-people bodies?"

"Exactly. I don't want to detract from the focus of our event by making it a heavy-handed 'statement.' It just seems right to showcase models with bodies that reflect reality."

"I dig that. Let's do it," Mona said with a fist pump. And every member of the design team echoed her sentiment.

"Wow, that was easy. You guys are awesome," Adelaide said with a broad smile. "Now let's get back to work."

Adelaide had some kinks to get out of last night's sketches before uploading them to her design program. Her excitement resurfaced as she worked on her design again. She didn't lift her head from her desk until her cell phone rang. It was Colin.

"Hey, cuz," she said, raising one arm over her head for a much-needed stretch. "What's up?"

"Do you want to meet up tonight? We haven't hung out properly in ages."

"I'd love to." Adelaide paused. They definitely needed to catch up, but she'd been counting the minutes until she saw Michael this evening. She looked around the now nearly empty studio and glanced at her watch. It was almost eight. Michael must be waiting. "But I can't tonight. I pulled an all-nighter last night and I'm about to keel over."

"You're boring when you're unconscious."

"Right? Will you be at Pendulum tomorrow night? I could come by the club with dinner," she offered, feeling guilty for ditching her cousin. But she needed to see Michael or she might go mad.

"Why don't you come by in a couple nights? I've been neglecting my clubs getting CS Productions off the ground. I'll be making the rounds at my other clubs tomorrow night."

"Got it. I'll see you soon then," she said, sounding sheepish.

"Yeah, catch you later."

As soon as they hung up, Adelaide texted Michael:

I didn't realize it was so late. I'm leaving the office now.

Her heart pounded with giddy excitement. She was going to be with him soon, but the impatience zooming through her insisted it wasn't soon enough.

*Oh, boy. I'm in so much trouble.*

Michael had been checking his phone for the eleventh time in the last ten minutes when it dinged with Adelaide's text. He sighed in relief. She would be here soon. It was nearly eight so the traffic shouldn't be horrendous. *Just hang on for thirty-five minutes, Reynolds.*

He was out of control. Knowing this had to end made him desperate to cherish every second with Adelaide. Stolen time. Time that shouldn't be his.

Michael couldn't give her children—her own family to cherish. And he refused to put her in the heartbreaking position of having to choose adoption or not having children. Even if she was willing to adopt in order to stay with him, her grandmother would never approve. Both James and Mrs. Song wanted grandchildren. If

Adelaide chose to be with him despite his infertility, it would create a rift between her and her family when she was so close to achieving her dream. He couldn't be the reason she lost her chance to work at Hansol— to head the sensory-friendly apparel line.

But he needed her. If they did everything right, he would still have the friendship of the Song family and his work to fill his days. But he needed Adelaide to warm his soul. He wanted to collect memories of her sweetness, her strength and her passion to carry with him once she was no longer his. That didn't make him any less of a selfish bastard.

His front door rang and Michael's heart thumped against his rib cage, but it was too soon for it to be Adelaide. It had only been five minutes since her text.

"Coming," he yelled as he took long strides toward the door. "Who is it?"

"It's Colin."

Michael yanked open the door to find that it was indeed Colin Song. Surprise staining his words, he asked, "What are you doing here?"

"I know it's been a while since I've dropped by, but I've come unannounced before. Why do you look so panicked?"

"I'm nothing of the sort, but like you said, it's been a long time," he said, bumping shoulders with his guest as they clapped each other's backs. "Come in."

They walked to the open kitchen, and Colin took a seat on the counter stool while Michael went around the island and reached into the fridge. "IPA or lager?"

"IPA," Colin replied, eyeing the champagne chilling

on ice on the counter. "Are you expecting company? A hot date?"

*Hell.* Adelaide. She would be here in less than half an hour. From Colin's teasing at the dinner with Mrs. Song, he already knew something was up between Michael and Adelaide. But Adelaide had wanted absolute secrecy, so Michael wasn't certain how she wanted to handle the situation with her cousin. Hopefully, he'd be able to send Colin off before Adelaide got here, but lying would only make things messier if they ran into each other tonight.

"Not exactly." He took a slow breath.

"Adelaide's the one coming over," Colin said in a solemn voice. "When will she be here?"

"Not for another thirty minutes," Michael admitted, eyeing the other man warily.

"Good. That'll give me plenty of time to say what I came here to say, then be out of your hair."

Michael paused with the beer halfway up to his mouth. He forced himself to take a sip and put the bottle down, pasting an easy grin on his face. "Well, that sounds intriguing. Let's hear it then."

"I know I'm younger than you and was a pesky kid that tagged along after you and Garrett."

"Wherever you're going with that, that was when we all were kids. Now you're nobody's tag-along."

"Good. Thanks for that, because you could think of me as Garrett's stand-in for what I'm about to say." Colin looked a little pained but determined. "I don't know how serious it is between you and Adelaide, but I want to know your intentions toward her."

"You what?" Michael didn't know whether to laugh or throw Colin out of the house.

"You're both adults and I don't want to interfere with your relationship." Colin held up his hand when Michael opened his mouth to interrupt. "And please don't bother denying there is anything between the two of you. This is uncomfortable enough as it is without me pointing out how obvious you guys are."

*Oh, hell. So much for discretion.*

"Look Mike, I don't think you realize how much Adelaide cares for you. She has hero-worshipped you since she was four, and she was crazy about you well into high school until you got married. She was devastated and heartbroken, and I thought she'd never be the same again. It wasn't a cute crush like people thought."

"I don't know what you're talking about."

"Then you're an idiot. Adelaide has been in love with you for years. When you got married, she tried to forget you by jumping from boyfriend to boyfriend. Her wild-girl years were her attempt to get over you because her heart refused to heal after your wedding. It took her a long time to get past her heartbreak and get her life back in order. Now she finally has this incredible opportunity to prove herself as the competent, brilliant woman she is. I can't stand by and do nothing when you have the power to ruin everything for her."

"I would never hurt her. In any way," Michael bit out, a muscle jumping in his jaw.

"Not intentionally. But if she falls in love with you and you break her heart again, I don't know what it would do to her."

"She's a grown woman who knows her own mind.

Neither you nor Garrett have a say in whom she decides to see." His hands fisted by his sides and he carefully unclenched them. "I understand that the older-brother syndrome turns you and Garrett into overbearing bastards, so I'll let this conversation slide. But if you ever attempt to interfere with our relationship again, I assure you I won't sit and listen politely."

"I hope never to have to say something like this again. It's not exactly my cup of tea. Besides, if I feel the need to interfere again, I doubt there will be much talking during the ass kicking."

Michael had to chuckle. Colin was dead serious. He didn't blame him, but he was way off the mark. Adelaide had never been in love with him. His chest tightened almost painfully at the thought, but he refused to entertain the possibility. She'd had a crush on him when she believed in unicorns and mermaids. He used to have a crush on his thirty-year-old nanny when he was that age.

"Are you finished with your male relative duties now? Because it looks like you and I need another bottle of beer."

"Yes, I'm done." Colin said, accepting another cold one. "And please don't tell Adelaide I said anything to you. She'd kill me if she found out."

"You sound pretty petrified. I'm surprised you took the risk of earning her wrath."

"Because I love her more than I fear her. But after Grandmother, Adelaide is the most badass human being in the world. Anyone with half a brain wouldn't mess with her."

The doorbell rang again, and both their eyes shot toward the main entrance. "Well, look at that. Adelaide is here early."

"Goddammit," Colin muttered. "Tell her I came over to talk to you about PR for my clubs."

"Like hell, I'm covering for you. I took your brow-beating like a gentleman, but the rest is up to you."

Michael left Colin mumbling curses under his breath to let Adelaide in. The sight of her took his breath away, and it took all his willpower not to kiss her senseless on his doorstep.

"Adelaide," he said in a low voice, stepping back to allow her in.

"Michael," she replied coyly, lifting up on her toes as though to kiss him.

He put a hand on her shoulder, shook his head and said rather loudly, "You wouldn't believe who's here, drinking my good beer."

She raised her eyebrows and mouthed, *Who?*

"Colin," he whispered. Then he said louder, "Let me show you who it is."

Adelaide tugged on his sleeve and whisper-screamed, "Oh, God. What's he doing here? He asked me out to dinner and I blew him off saying I pulled an all-nighter. What is he going to think?"

"He's going to think I insisted you visit despite your fatigue so we could celebrate your ingenious design ideas."

"Colin already knows. He would never breathe a word of it to anyone, but I'm not ready to talk to anyone about us. I want it to be our secret only. I don't want to share a single slice of it."

She was too adorable to resist, and he kissed her hard before stepping back quickly.

"I needed that," she said, sounding winded. "Okay. Let's all go ignore the elephant in the room."

When they arrived at the kitchen, Colin half stood from his counter stool and gave Adelaide a hug. "Fancy meeting you here, cuz."

"I'm so glad we all ended up here tonight. We can have a hearty dinner and talk business before I collapse."

"Who said I had enough for our uninvited guest?" Michael half teased. He wanted Adelaide to himself, and frustration threatened to darken his mood. "I'll butterfly the steak for the three of us to share, and grill some shrimp on the side."

Adelaide sat to his right during dinner, and he could feel the heat coming off her. He needed to bring up his deepest reserve of self-control in order not to touch her under the table, because he didn't want to disrespect Colin after their talk. But he did lightly squeeze her knee to let her know he wanted her. She ran her hands down his thigh in response, and he almost choked on his steak.

"You okay, Mike?" Colin asked with concern.

"I'm fine," he answered, taking two big gulps of wine.

The cause of his troubles ducked her head to her plate and stuffed shrimp in her mouth to hide her smirk. *Mischievous little fox.*

When the excitement settled—only to half-mast for Michael—the dinner conversation turned naturally toward the fashion show.

"My design team has a little less than a month to turn in their final designs," Adelaide said. "I don't know how I'll choose one of them as the winner when they're all so amazing."

"That sounds tough," said Colin. "I have good news for you, though. I heard back from some of my DJ friends, and they would love to attend the charity event."

"Oh, my gosh. That's incredible news," she gushed. "Some of them are big-name artists. The online audience will go through the roof."

"It's going to be a fantastic event." Colin smiled.

"Thank you," said Adelaide, with affection lighting up her lovely face.

"Good work, Colin." Michael nodded in approval. "Anyone need a refill?"

"I think we're all a bite away from bursting. Right?" Colin answered then turned to Adelaide. "I'll drive you home then take a taxi back to pick up my car. You okay with that, Mike?"

"Of course." Like hell he was. The conniving little bastard was playing chaperon again, and there was no way out of it that wouldn't look suspicious.

"What? I—" Adelaide protested.

"You pulled an all-nighter last night, and had two glasses of wine. I'm not letting you drive home."

"I could drive her—" Michael said in a last-ditch effort.

"With all due respect, you look like you haven't slept in a week yourself. I'll take her home and you get some rest. Sorry I can't stay to help you clean up, but she looks like she's about to face-plant into the shrimp tails."

Adelaide huffed beside him but stayed quiet otherwise. They both knew Colin was on to them.

"Thanks, Colin." Admitting defeat, Michael followed the two Songs to the door. "Drive safe."

"Will do." With a handshake and a forearm bump, Colin walked toward Adelaide's car, giving them a minute. That was decent of him.

"I can't believe he's chaperoning me!" She blew up as soon as he was out of earshot.

"Can you expect any less from a Song male?" Michael teased, tucking a strand of hair behind her ear. She shivered at his touch, and sighed deep and long.

"Phone sex in an hour?" She wiggled her eyebrows.

"Don't tease," he groaned. "But Colin's right. We both need rest. I'll see you tomorrow, okay?"

"Fine. Tomorrow," she sighed, and gave him two lingering kisses on the corners of his mouth.

"Go," he said hoarsely. "While I can let you go."

# Eleven

"It's good to hear your voice, baby."

The butterflies in Adelaide's stomach launched into flight. It was hard to believe Michael was saying these words to her. Her dearest friend. Her forever crush. Her soul flushed with shy pleasure, then flooded with the sounds of the universal language of love—Puccini. One sleepy-voiced sentence was all it took.

*Wait. Love?*

There was no love. This wasn't forever. She'd drawn a firm line between them. This would be over once the fashion show ended. She couldn't let her relationship with Michael become the center of her world. Her grandmother was seeing the tip of her potential, but that was only the beginning. She had so much more in her. Adelaide couldn't lose sight of that even for a little while. Her fling with Michael was just that—a fling. She couldn't risk her future on a man who only had *now* to offer.

"Imagine how good it would be to see me in person," she quipped with false bravado.

"You really want to put me through this first thing in the morning?"

She laughed, feeling a bit abashed for calling him the moment she had opened her eyes that morning. But she wasn't trying to turn him on or anything. Well, maybe a little. "I just wanted to hear your voice, too. And to invite you to come with me to my meeting with the set designers. Your presence isn't strictly necessary, but I miss you."

The silence from his end of the line seemed to stretch on. "I...can't. It seems my more impulsive clients need my attention today. I swear they're giving me premature grays."

"Oh, of course. You do have a company to run." Adelaide did her best to hide the disappointment in her voice. "Will I see you tonight? Without Colin?"

"I would love to, but I have to see how my day goes." Michael's chuckle sounded stilted. "I'll call you later."

"Okay. Talk to you soon."

"Bye."

Adelaide moved like a robot through her morning routine to get herself ready for work. When she went down to the kitchen, her grandmother was already finishing her coffee and half a buttered bagel—her go-to weekday breakfast.

"Good morning, *Hal-muh-nee*."

"Come and eat. You look thin."

"I'm just tired. I had to work straight through the night a couple days ago, and I'm still recovering."

"Ah, yes. The passion of youth." She smiled with a faraway look.

Adelaide felt her face redden with guilt at her grandmother's unintentional innuendo. *The passion of youth, indeed.* "What are your plans for the day?"

"I'm meeting with some board members for lunch. I need to see them in person to get an accurate read on their positions on the Hansol-Vivotex partnership. They praise Garrett to the heavens when I'm on the phone with them, but I need to make certain the board members aren't just kissing my ass." She snorted, sounding incredibly poised, even arrogant. *I so want to be like you when I grow up.* "It'll be good for you to remember that, Adelaide. Never take what you hear at face value. You need to decipher the truth through your gut instinct."

"I'll remember it well," she replied, her jaw gaping loose. This was the first time her grandmother had ever given her words of wisdom about running the company. The validation and genuine counsel made her dizzy with pride. And it reinforced her earlier resolve that her relationship with Michael couldn't become a distraction. It would be a disaster if Grandmother ever found out about their fling. She had to make doubly sure that it was a very short and discreet affair.

The sense of acceptance and pride stayed with her as she drove to her meeting, but so did her phone call with Michael. She replayed their conversation in her mind. He was flirtatious and sexy until the moment she told him she missed him. It couldn't be. Did those simple words convince him that she was becoming too attached? They'd had one night together. Did he think it'd been too much for little Adelaide? She couldn't stop the insecurities flooding her mind.

After a few missed turns, she arrived at the loft to meet with the set designers so they could take the necessary measurements to create a runway suited for the space and theme. She compartmentalized her dizzying feelings and allowed her mind to focus fully on the business at hand.

Once she got back to her car, the dam she'd built around her worries crumbled to the ground. Adelaide reached for her phone but pulled her hand back. What would she say? *Do you still want me?* She was being ridiculous. Hadn't she decided not to let their fling distract her? They shouldn't spend every night together.

Besides, the way he'd made love to her couldn't have been her imagination. He'd taken her as though they were the only two beings left on earth and he'd been looking a lifetime for her. Michael wanted her. Even if it was short-term—even if it was just sex—he wanted her desperately. And she was happy with that. That was all she wanted, as well. To burn through the magnetic chemistry between them. She needed to stop analyzing his every word and action.

Adelaide took a deep breath and let her anxiety go. She drove out of her spot on the street and headed back to the office. It was already late afternoon, but she had to put together a cohesive vision of the theme she wanted the set designers to execute, and have it to them in the next couple days.

Her cell phone dinged in her purse and her anxiety returned full force. Where had all her hard-won confidence and maturity gone? Was she back to craving constant affection so she could feel wanted? She wasn't going back. She didn't need any man—including Michael Reynolds—to feel valued.

Adelaide didn't bother checking her text. It was most likely the designers she'd met asking her for some clarifications. Only when she returned to her desk did she pull out her phone. She was proud to have her self-confidence and control back. Unfortunately, the message she found didn't please her.

The issue with my problem client isn't as simple to solve as I'd thought. Sorry. I'm going to have to take a rain check on tonight.

She forced back the panicked thoughts crowding her mind. She was fine with not seeing Michael for one night. He wasn't the center of her world.

No worries. Good luck with putting out the fire.

The ellipses appeared on the screen as though Michael was typing a response, but soon it stopped without a text from him. Again. She refused to sweat it. He probably got pulled away.

Despite her determination to not fret over not seeing Michael, she didn't want to head home for a quiet night. It had been forever since she'd danced the night away. In fact, she hadn't been to her cousin's club since that night Michael showed up to *escort* her home.

Suddenly she wanted to get out of the office. Letting go of the stress of the past few days by losing herself to music and dancing sounded like exactly what she needed. But she wanted some fun, uncomplicated company. She took a sweeping glance around the studio and found her favorite team members, Mona and Chris.

"Okay, team. I won't take no for an answer. Let's go dancing!"

Mona shot to her feet gratifyingly fast and whooped, "Let's go par-tay."

"Well, you don't need to twist my arm," Chris chimed in. "I'll text Cindy to join us."

"Good call, Chris." Adelaide fist-bumped Chris. She sensed a blooming romance between them, and it was so sweet. She was their matchmaker in a way. "Hey, Mona. Let's go raid the sample racks in the women's department for some cocktail dresses. Chris, you wanna hit up the men's department?"

"Heck, yeah."

"Do you want to knock the socks off your girl and go with something other than flannel for our night out?" she teased.

"I don't know about that." He narrowed his eyes and rubbed his beard in contemplation.

"Well, why don't you surprise us?" Mona said.

"Deal. Makeover time, ladies." Chris was out the door faster than them.

Adelaide was in the mood for something festive and sparkly, so she chose a strapless midlength gold sequin dress that hugged her body without holding back. She chose crystal drop earrings that dangled just shy of her shoulders, and strappy crystal-studded shoes. She kind of looked like Lumière from *Beauty and the Beast*, and she loved it.

"Oh, my gosh, Mona." The designer was stunning in a red off-the-shoulder A-line dress that accentuated her hourglass figure, and her four-inch stiletto heels made her look like an Amazonian badass. "You look hot. And I mean that in the most respectful and professional sense."

"Oh, forget professionalism. I know you aren't hitting on me," she laughed delightedly. "You just can't contain your awe at my eat-your-heart-out dress."

"So true, girlfriend."

Mona had the perfect universal bloodred lipstick that they both put on and went down to the lobby to meet up with Chris. They almost walked past a tall, fit man checking his cell phone, wearing a tight black dress shirt and charcoal leather pants with a bold silver-buckled belt. But the man lifted his head to reveal his bearded face just before they passed him.

"Chris?" Adelaide and Mona both asked at once.

"What? Do I look different or something?" He grinned broadly.

"Cindy is a lucky girl. That's all I have to say," Mona said with a low whistle.

Chris turned adorably red and volunteered to be the designated driver. When they got to the club, there was a good crowd, but it wasn't suffocating since it was a weeknight. Clarence, Tucker's apprentice, was helming the mixer tonight, and the music pumped through Adelaide's veins with the perfect amount of power and spice.

"Hey, Adelaide," Tucker met them near the entrance. "It's been too long. Let me set you and your friends up. Colin isn't here tonight. You knew that, right?"

"Yup. Why do you think I chose tonight to come?"

Adelaide joked with a wink. "Guys, this is Tucker, the manager and the best DJ on Pendulum's roster. Tucker, this is Chris and Mona. A beautiful young woman named Cindy will be joining us soon, so be on the lookout for her please."

Once everyone had said their hellos, Tucker set them up at a great table with a bottle of blanco tequila and a mountain of limes.

"Is there anything else you need?" he asked.

"Nah, we're set. Thanks." She high-fived him, and the rest of the table nodded profusely, grinning ear to ear. "Okay. Two shots to get us started, then we hit the dance floor."

"You got it, girl," Mona shouted over the music.

As soon as Adelaide's strappy heals hit the dance floor, Clarence filled the air with her favorite songs. It wasn't long before the music formed a layer of invisible skin around her, and her movements felt as though she was floating in water. Her blood hummed with elation, and she closed her eyes and surrendered herself to the sensations. She and Mona shared Chris, who was an exceptionally good dancer, until Cindy joined them in the chicest, hottest pink jumpsuit, and then he was all hers.

The four of them finished the bottle of tequila and burned off all the alcohol on the dance floor. Mona shouted for another bottle, but Adelaide had to be the big, bad boss and put on the breaks.

"I'm calling it a night. We'll have a flowing supply of tequila once the fashion show is finished, but it's past one o'clock. I don't want you missing class or half-assing on the fashion show prep tomorrow."

"Boo," Mona said. She was so cute all tipsy.

"Thank you, Adelaide," Cindy and Chris said in chorus, their hands linked.

Adelaide stepped outside while the rest of the crew got their things together. The chill in the night air was welcome against her heated skin, and she inhaled a deep, cleansing breath. The breath caught in her throat when a hand grabbed her purse.

"Hey!" she said, holding on to the straps. "Let. Go."

The purse snatcher bared his teeth, slammed his shoulder into her and knocked her to the ground. The pain and shock of being hit cut off her air supply, and Adelaide curled up into a ball on the ground. As she drew in a full breath, a pair of strong arms wrapped around her shoulders and gently sat her up. She struggled against the hold for a brief moment until a voice broke through her whimpering.

"Adelaide, it's me. It's Chris. Don't worry." He held her tight and patted her back gently. "You're safe now."

The assailant had taken her purse, along with her phone. She had to pull herself together and make sure he didn't get access to her texts with Michael. But she was frightened, and her body felt like a giant bruise.

"Oh, my God!" Cindy and Mona rushed to her side. "Are you okay?"

"I'm fine. Only a little shaken." With the help of her friends, she got to her feet and dusted herself off. There was no time for her to be shaking with fear. She had to make sure the theft of her phone didn't escalate into catastrophe. "I need to borrow one of your phones."

Jealousy wasn't an emotion familiar to him, but when Michael's media alert chimed at four in the morning, he was filled with the toxic green fume. A picture of Adelaide dancing seductively a few inches from Chris. Another shot of her in Chris's arms, clinging to the front of his shirt. He wasn't fully awake, but he wanted to beat the hell out of the design student.

Then the headline caught his attention and brought him fully awake: Adelaide Song Involved in a Love Affair with her Student Employee.

What the hell was going on? He scrolled down to find additional pictures. Adelaide was in Chris's arms, but she was sitting smack in the middle of the sidewalk. In the next picture, she was standing with Chris, Cindy and Mona. In the background of the picture, Tucker and some bouncers hovered around them with fierce expressions.

Had something happened to Adelaide? His world seemed to compress around him. Nothing else mattered but her. She had to be safe. *Goddammit*. None of this would've happened if he hadn't canceled their date last night.

It was true he'd had fires to put out, but his canceling was partly motivated by his guilt and fear. When she'd told him she missed him, Michael thought his heart would burst from happiness. Then he recalled Colin's warning. What if she believed she was falling in love with him? That meant he could break her heart by leaving her, and he would rather die than hurt her. But staying with her wasn't an option. She deserved better.

His feelings for Adelaide had overwhelmed him. Michael had told himself they needed some space to get their emotions in check, but as soon as he told her he couldn't see her, he regretted his cowardly move. She was the one who'd wanted the two-month affair. If she was falling in love with him, she would've told him she'd changed her mind. Right?

But now she could be hurt somewhere because he wasn't there for her. If she was getting rest after an ordeal, Michael didn't want to wake her. But there was no chance in hell he'd fall back asleep not knowing whether she was okay.

If Tucker and the bouncers were around, then she'd obviously been at Pendulum. He had no qualms about waking up Colin. Michael was going insane with worry.

"Colin."

"What the hell, Mike? I got to bed an hour ago. Call me back tomorrow."

"I'll come pound on your door if you hang up on me. Where's Adelaide? Is she okay?"

"How do you know about that? Hell, is it all over the media already?"

"Screw the media. How is Adelaide? Tell me, goddammit."

"Calm down. She's okay. She has some scrapes and bruises, but she's strong. She handled herself like a soldier during the police interview. You couldn't have guessed she'd been assaulted half an hour before that."

"Assaulted? Police interview?" Michael had been pacing his room, but he sat back on his bed when his knees nearly gave out. "Start from the beginning. All I saw was a picture of her sitting on the sidewalk clinging to Chris like she was terrified."

"Right." Colin sighed, and seemed to shake the sleep off of himself. "I think she put together a night out for some of her designers. According to Tucker, they were a fun group and seemed to have a great time until Adelaide put the brakes on them around one o'clock. She was lecturing them about having to work the next day. Responsibility is making her boring."

Michael huffed a tense laugh at Colin's attempt to lighten his anxiety. "So boring."

"Yeah, I know. Well, she went out of the club before the rest of her group, and some bastard tried to snatch her purse. And of course, our Adelaide fought him off, playing tug-of-war with her purse with her much bigger assailant. Finally, he slammed his shoulder into her and knocked her to the ground, and took off with her purse." Colin didn't wait for Michael to respond. "At any rate, it seems he'd been hanging around outside the club for easy targets. He grabbed Adelaide before anyone else came out, but Chris heard her scream and the other designers got Tucker and our men."

Michael's vision blurred and the room glowed faintly red as fury trembled inside him like a volcano about to erupt. "What happened to the assailant?"

"Long gone. Adelaide didn't get a good look at him. He wore a cap lowered over his eyes."

"Hell." He rubbed his face wearily. "What about Adelaide? Has she been seen by a doctor? Is she home now?"

"Yes, the paramedics checked her out. They said she's pretty bruised up on her ribs from the hit, and her arms, legs and hip from the fall. Thankfully, she didn't hit her head on the sidewalk. I want to kill the bastard."

Michael couldn't speak for a moment as he envisioned Adelaide's injuries. Angry dark bruises and scrapes all over her body. And bruised ribs? He flung his pillow across the room and knocked down a lamp.

"Mike!" Colin seemed startled by the crash. "I need you to calm down. You have to focus on the fact that she is safe and sound."

"Having bruised ribs because someone *hit* her is *not* safe and sound," he gritted through his teeth.

"God, you're acting crazier than Garrett. Maybe he was toning things down not to freak out his pregnant wife and toddler, but come on, Mike. You're going to give yourself a stroke."

"You already told Garrett?" He knew it wasn't Colin's fault, but his anger was surging out of his pores. "Were you ever planning on telling me?"

"I understand you're in shock, but you need to back the hell up. She's my cousin. And because she's my dear cousin, I kept my promise to her that I'd let her tell you."

The pressure building up inside of him seemed to fizzle and deflate. "Adelaide told you not to tell me."

"She wanted to tell you when she felt more herself. Give her some time to rest, and I'm sure she'll call you in the morning. When the sun's up. Like normal people do."

"Hell. I'm sorry, man. I lost it for a second." Michael wiped his hand down his face. "Thank you for taking care of her."

"I'm just sorry I wasn't there when it happened. I was at another club but got there as soon as I could."

"You did your best. Thanks, again."

"Of course. Try to get some rest."

"I will. I hope you can go back to sleep."

"Ha! You're not getting off that easily. You owe me a drink, Reynolds."

"Definitely. Good night."

He hung up his phone and headed for the shower. There was no chance he was getting another wink of sleep until he saw for himself that Adelaide was okay. After a hot shower to restore his equilibrium, he was going to find the media outlet that had published the incendiary article and shut them down.

Michael waited all day for Adelaide's call, but there was only radio silence. When he spoke with Liliana in the morning, she said Adelaide had gone into work after speaking with Mrs. Song. He wished she'd taken a day off to recuperate, but maybe she needed to lose herself in work to forget about her ordeal.

In the early morning, he had extinguished the tabloid article before it could spread wide. Chris had been helping her after a mobbing as reported to the police. The tabloid's claim of a relationship between Chris and Adelaide was libelous, pure and simple. He used the existence of a police report, and the clout of his firm and Hansol Corporation to force the tabloid trash to make nice and withdraw the article immediately. They were to respond to any inquiries by saying it was an unsubstantiated story and had therefore been withdrawn. He just hoped he got it done before Mrs. Song got wind of it. A scandal like this could impact the respect and trust that Adelaide had built up between them.

By the time six o'clock rolled around, he couldn't stay away a second longer, so he marched into her studio. He froze midstride when he spotted Adelaide sketching at her desk.

"Adelaide." His voice broke over her name.

Her head shot up and her mask of serenity cracked. Her trembling hand rose to her mouth as tears filled her eyes, and he ran to her and enveloped her in his arms. The studio was thankfully empty.

"Shh, baby. You're okay." He wiped away the tears trailing down her face and pressed featherlight kisses on her lips. Again and again. Telling her as well as himself that she was okay. "I'm here."

Slowly the tremors eased from her body, and she melted against him, limp and spent. "Take me home."

She didn't need to ask him twice or explain to him that she meant his house, not hers. Once they were out of the studio, Michael replaced his tight grip around her shoulders with a light touch at her lower back. Adelaide walked, her face a picture of calm confidence. She even remembered to sling her laptop bag over her shoulder. The Song family control was legendary for a reason.

Once she was ensconced in the front seat of his sedan, Adelaide dropped her mask, leaned her head against his shoulder and closed her eyes. Michael backed his car out carefully, putting his arm around her to hold her steady.

The traffic was relatively light, and he was soon pulling the car into his driveway. Holding her against his body, he walked her into the house. Adelaide's hands were cold and the pallor of her lips matched the creamy skin of her face, which held no hint of color. She hadn't said a word during the drive, and he didn't ask a single question. She would talk when she was ready.

"Come here." He led her to his bed and laid her down over the covers, adjusting the pillows around her. "Let me draw you a bath. You need to get warm."

Her lashes fluttered shut as though she was exhausted. When Colin spoke of Adelaide's strength last night, Michael knew she had held her own with iron will, but he also knew that she was compartmentalizing all her fear and emotions in order to present an unshakable front. She needed a release to process everything she had bottled up inside. He intended to hold her through it all.

Michael never had women over at his house and regretted not having any fragrant bubbles for her bath. The best he could do for her was fill the deep tub with warm water and light some candles he'd gotten as a Christmas present last year. He was pleasantly surprised to find the scent of jasmine filling his bathroom. It was Adelaide's favorite.

When it was ready, he sat her up on his bed and began to undress her. She wore a dress shirt buttoned up to her neck and a beige pencil skirt. Too toned down for her usual style. As he undid the buttons of her shirt, his gut wrenched painfully. Angry dark blue bruises spanned her chest and ribs, and helpless fury shook him from head to toe.

"Hush," Adelaide said, smoothing his hair from his forehead and kissing him sweetly. "I'm okay, Michael."

"I know." He couldn't fall apart right now. She needed him to be strong for her.

After he finished undressing her, he gathered her in his arms and eased her into the bathtub. She didn't say another word, but her eyes didn't leave his as he washed her like a child. She looked as though she was assuring herself that he was real.

"I'm here. You're safe now."

He washed every inch of her with reverence, silently telling her how much he cherished her. Then he gently dried her off and pulled one of his T-shirts over her head before tucking her under the covers. He lay down beside her over the covers and slid his arm around her so her head rested on his chest.

"Rest now, baby." The first heart-wrenching sob escaped her then. He wrapped his other arm around her and crushed her flush against his body. "Let it all out."

He held her tight and rode out the storm until her tears soaked through his shirt. After long minutes, her sobs subsided. Then her tears dried up, and the painful knot in Michael's stomach eased. He kissed the top of her head and drew circles on her back until she fell asleep. He hoped she'd found her peace and was ready to take the first step toward putting the nightmare behind her.

He studied her sleeping face and noticed how angelic and vulnerable she looked. The asshole had hit her and knocked her to the ground. Michael felt the growl build in his chest, a raw, feral sound. He wanted to tear the bastard apart with his bare hands. Adelaide stirred in his arms, and Michael bit back the anger spilling over him. His anger was his to deal with, and not what Adelaide needed right now.

He inhaled deep breaths through his nose and steadied his heartbeat. He would be whoever she wanted him to be when she woke up. The person who could help her process the events of the night before. Someone who could make her smile. And if she wanted, someone who could make love to her until she forgot everything.

# Twelve

When she woke up a couple hours later, she felt the warmth of Michael's arm around her. She felt safe and whole again. But when she saw him, awake and staring unblinkingly at the ceiling, she realized how shaken he was by what had happened to her.

Either Garrett or Colin had filled him in. That much was obvious. And it was a relief to know that she wouldn't have to talk about it in any detail with him. Even the thought of reliving the incident made her nauseous. But she desperately wanted to erase the haunted look on his face, which was probably a reflection of her own expression.

"Hi," she whispered, tilting her head up.

"Hi, yourself." He immediately raised himself on his elbow and gazed at her face. Unwrapping his arm from her, he cupped her face in one hand, looking at her with such tenderness that her heart melted. "How are you feeling?"

"Limp. In the best kind of way. Like I had the most relaxing massage in the world."

"Good. Did you sleep well?"

"Like a rock." She smiled, surprised at how much she was enjoying Michael's doting. She didn't know if he realized it, but he seemed to need to take care of her as much as she needed him to.

"Are you hungry? I could make you some pasta." He moved as if to get up from bed, and Adelaide snatched at his arm.

"No. I'm not hungry for pasta," she said, sliding her hand down his arm when he stopped pushing himself up. "But I am starving for you."

"Adelaide…" He sounded choked. "We don't need to do anything."

"Oh, but we do. I need you more than anything right now." She sat up and pushed Michael down flat on his back, and started undoing the buttons of his shirt. "Please make love to me. Make me feel safe."

He nodded and lay still under her impatient hands. His jaws clenched when she parted his shirt and smoothed her hands over his chest and stomach. Still he didn't move, instead giving her full control. She moved down to his pants. First she unbuckled his belt. Then she unbuttoned and unzipped his pants, and pulled them off him with a strong tug. His hard length strained against his boxer briefs, so she relieved him of those as well.

When he was finally naked, she pulled her shirt off, threw it carelessly behind her and straddled him. They both moaned and moved restlessly at the contact. She lifted her hips up to rub her aching bud against his length and leaned forward to place her breasts in front of his face.

"Take me in your mouth," she demanded.

When he complied without hesitation, she screamed at the intense pleasure, her hips bucking against him for more friction. Her movements became frantic as he suckled her, and he grabbed her behind to move her against him. She was slick with desire, and so close.

Hearing the change in her breathing, Michael slid his finger into her as she continued to stimulate her clit against his hardness. He added a second finger inside her, then scraped the peak of her breast with his teeth hard enough to make her gasp. All his touches combined threw her into the waves of her passion, and her climax crashed into her.

Michael tore open a condom and flipped her onto her back. In one swift move, he pushed into her and rode her into another orgasm before she could come down from her first one. She screamed his name and met him push for push.

"I'm yours, Adelaide," he said, thrusting into her without finesse, without control. "I'll be everything you need me to be."

"You already are."

At her breathless words, he pumped into her one last time and shouted hoarsely as he found his own release. As they floated down to earth and sweat began to dry on their skin, he still didn't pull away from her. He just turned them over to their sides and hung on to her. She was more than happy to stay connected to him.

"Are you okay?" he asked, tenderly tucking a strand of hair behind her ear.

"I'm better than okay." She smiled lazily at him.

"God, Adelaide. I'm so sorry I wasn't there with you last night."

"Michael." She cupped the side of his face. "It wasn't your fault. You can't let what happened eat away at you. It's not worth it. Let's both let it go."

"You're right. It's in the past." Then, with a teasing tone, he said, "But if something like this ever happens again, please let them take the goddamn purse."

She sighed and kissed him sweetly. "Got it. It's gonna take a while for these bruises to go away. Definitely not worth it."

"Did Mrs. Song tell you anything this morning?" he asked hesitantly.

"You mean about the tabloid article?"

"You know about it? How did you see it? It should've been all gone."

"No, I didn't see it, but Grandmother has scary fast intel. She saw it," Adelaide said.

"Was she…upset with you?"

"That's the thing. She wasn't upset at all. First, she fussed over me and made sure I was okay. Then she told me about the article. She said she only wanted me to be aware of it, and that you would take care of it. Grandmother didn't believe a word of it. She really trusts me."

"Way to go, Grandma Grace."

"I can't believe you just called her that." She giggled, burying her face in his neck.

He laughed with her until a quiet calm settled around them. Then he noticed her bruises again, and ran his hand down the side of her body. "Are you sure you're okay?"

"That was mind-blowing, bone-melting sex for the ages," she quipped. "Can't you see I'm thoroughly satiated after two rounds of orgasm?"

"Satiated?"

Adelaide briefly regretted her praise when Michael's grin grew arrogant and predatory. Then again, arrogant and predatory turned her on.

"Mind-blowing and bone-melting, huh?" he persisted.

"Well, I was exaggerating a bit about being satiated. There is always room for improvement."

"Is that so, you little fox?" Her eyes rounded when she felt him growing hard again inside her. "Ready for a new and improved round then? I can't let you leave the bed unsatisfied."

"But… I thought you said…it hasn't been two hours yet." She squirmed out of his reach, not sure she had another orgasm in her. She was spent from the other two he had given her just minutes ago.

"Desperate times call for desperate measures and all that." He reached for a tissue box to clean himself off and pulled on a second condom. "My body can't rest until it satiates yours."

"I'm satiated. I'm satiated!" She yelped and tried to jump out of bed, but Michael grabbed her with lightning speed and gently pushed her back down on the bed.

"Not so fast. I want you to say that when I'm taking you hard and fast. Would you like that?"

Adelaide suddenly went limp, her center getting

slippery with renewed passion. "Yes. Please and thank you."

They reached for each other more desperately than the first time. Feral and wild. She dug her nails into his back. She bit him. Adelaide marked him as hers. And when they came together shouting each other's names, her walls crumbled and fell, leaving her heart bare and raw.

*I love you.*

Who had said that? Was it him? Or her? Or had he imagined it? The words floated in the thick air that smelled of sex and sweat.

He couldn't be in love with her. Even he wasn't so much of a masochist. He wouldn't give his heart to a woman he could never have. The one woman he didn't deserve to love. But if she had said the words… His heart filled with a joy so blinding he thought he could fly. But he came crashing down in milliseconds. She couldn't love him.

*But don't you remember Colin's warning? She loved you once. Why can't she love you again?*

Because she couldn't. He couldn't bear to hurt her. He had to end things before she got too attached. It couldn't be love. But if she was already in love with him, he'd be breaking her heart no matter what.

It couldn't be true. He couldn't hurt her or end things with her right now. They had close to a month left until the fashion show and he would hold on to her until the last minute. *Wait.* Adelaide was just recovering from a traumatic experience. He was familiar. He was safe. If she had indeed said those words, they were born from fatigue and relief.

They weren't in love. They were just two very lucky people who had incredible chemistry. He'd experienced the best sex of his life with her, but that wasn't love. The same had be true for her. He needed to stop being so dramatic and enjoy the time they had together.

They fell asleep in each other's arm for a sweet cat-nap and woke up close to midnight.

"That pasta sounds fantastic right now," she said, stretching languidly beside him. *Thank God.* The whole "I love you" thing had been a hallucination. She was acting like nothing had changed. *Good.* That was good.

Michael ran his hands down the length of her torso and grabbed her round ass. But before he exhausted both of them further, he jumped out of bed and stepped into his boxers.

"Coming right up. Spaghetti puttanesca, okay?"

"Yum. It sounds delicious and…satisfying."

Michael lunged for the siren, but she rolled away from him and locked herself in his bathroom. Her laughter rang through the door, and color burst through his life, making his world HD clear and spectacular.

It was just the two of them in their haven, and the events of the night before became insignificant specks of dust.

For the next few weeks, Michael and Adelaide got into a beautiful rhythm where they each worked hard during the day, then spent the evenings together— mostly at his place for privacy. But they never spent the entire night in each other's arms, which ate away at him. They had to double up in their efforts to be discreet with their affair after what had happened at the club with Chris.

Mrs. Song had invited him to dinner tonight at the Song residence, so he was braving the rush hour traffic to Pacific Palisades. Even though they would have Adelaide's toughest chaperones eyeing them like hawks—James Song was back from his trip to New York—Michael's heart thrummed out a bruising beat against his ribs at the prospect of seeing her.

Michael's desire for her only grew day by day. He had a sinking feeling that there was no getting her out of his system. In all honesty, he couldn't even feign surprise over that. He had known all along. But his desire for her had grown stronger than he had ever thought possible. She was like an addiction that he never wanted to be free of.

Liliana greeted him at the door with a warm smile and patted him on the back. "It's lovely to have you here, Michael. Mr. Song can't wait to share his adventures in New York with you. Apparently, Sophie dyed a patch of his hair orange. Go ask him how."

"I'll do that." He laughed, taking his shoes off to enter the house. "I brought some *dduk* and fermented rice drink."

"Ooh, rice cake and *shik-heh*."

"Yeah, that." That was the one Korean word that Michael had the most trouble pronouncing. At one point, he decided to stop embarrassing himself and used the English description of the dessert drink. He still practiced the word in private since it was one of Adelaide's favorite drinks.

When he saw Adelaide walking down the hallway toward him, his breath hitched. She had her hair in a ponytail and wore a pair of slim black jeans and a loose T-shirt. She would be enchanting in a potato sack.

"Hi," he said in a rush of breath. She smiled widely at him, her lovely eyes becoming crescent moons. They both jumped when Liliana coughed quietly.

"Let me take those from you, Michael. I'll put the *shik-heh* in the fridge."

"Ooh, you brought *shik-heh*?" Adelaide bounced on her toes. "Thank you, Michael. That sounds amazing."

"I'll put a bowl in the freezer so it gets icy at the top, just the way you like it," Liliana said with a wink.

"You're the best. Thank you."

As soon as the housekeeper walked away with the bounty, Adelaide jumped on him and showered kisses on his face.

"Whoa," he said, kissing her back smooch for smooch, and not doing anything to stop her. "Slow down. What if someone sees?"

Adelaide finally eased up and placed a lazy kiss on his lips before pulling away. "Chicken."

"Yes. Yes, I am." He grinned, but after looking to make sure no one was near, he kissed her hard. "One last kiss to make sure I don't look at you like I want you for dessert all throughout the meal."

"I don't know, Reynolds. You always look at me like I'm an ice-cream cone on a hot day on the boardwalk."

"Yes, because I want to lick you and devour you until you fall apart in my arms."

"That is not fair," she groaned. "I can't even leave

with you tonight. Dad will moan and groan about not seeing me for weeks if I try to go out."

"Sorry, but if it makes you feel any better, the torture is equally real for me."

"I missed you today," she whispered, taking a step back to create a respectable distance between them. "And I'll miss you tonight."

And because he couldn't help the words from spilling from his heart, he said, "I'll miss you more."

They walked to the kitchen to find both the elder Songs already seated at the table.

"Mrs. Song." Michael bowed once at the waist and again toward Adelaide's dad. "James."

"Good to see you, son," James replied jovially. Michael felt guilt churn in his stomach and averted his eyes.

"Have a seat, Michael," Mrs. Song instructed. "We don't want our food getting cold."

"Yes, ma'am."

He stole a glance at Adelaide and found her eyes lowered to the table. It had never been this hard to be around her family before they'd slept together. Now he felt like an unruly teenager trying to behave at the table. They definitely wouldn't be playing footsies.

Liliana's cooking was amazing as usual, and dinner progressed with casual conversation and James's anecdotes from his trip to New York.

"Michael." The Song matriarch addressed him with gravitas. His heart jumped to his throat. He needed to calm the hell down. She didn't know about them. "That ridiculous article about Adelaide and one of her designers has been wiped clean from what I could see. I believe I have you to thank for that."

"It was my pleasure," he replied with feeling. "Those bastards—pardon the language—were targeting Adelaide's reputation. That is unacceptable, especially this close to the fashion show."

"Yes. With the fashion show only a week away, we have to be extra vigilant about our conduct. Rumors and scandal that make her look irresponsible would be a big blow to the event." Mrs. Song nodded solemnly. "I trust you to continue assisting Adelaide and protecting her. Thank you for your hard work."

"You're very welcome, Mrs. Song." Michael took a sip of water and coughed into his fist. *Damn*. The guilt was killing him, but his time with Adelaide was precious. He didn't regret a single minute and would cherish every remaining second.

"Adelaide, I trust I don't have to remind you of how important your reputation is at this crucial time," Mrs. Song said to her granddaughter.

"Of course, Grandmother," Adelaide said quietly. She snuck a look at Michael and quickly brought her gaze down to her hands. "This project means the world to me. I won't do anything to jeopardize it."

Adelaide was right. They weren't seen together in public unless it was related to the charity, and they hadn't spent a long stretch of time together since her assault. They were fully aware of the risk they were taking and took extra measures to be completely discreet.

Since they avoided eye contact throughout dinner, Michael did an excellent job of not looking at Adelaide like she was dessert. But he felt her nearness like a caress across his skin. Even though guilt burned through him, he couldn't let her go a minute too early. He still had a week left with his lovely Adelaide, and he wasn't thinking about the end until the end.

# Thirteen

Adelaide stared down at her sketch pad and listlessly drew the outline of a figure. She had no more clothes to design with the event less than a week away. Her team's designs were complete, and the contest winner had been selected. It'd taken Adelaide many sleepless nights to come to her final decision. Chris's royal blue slacks and vest set was absolutely gorgeous. And she was in love with so many of the evening gowns that she wanted to own them all. But in the end, Mona won the summer internship with her slim rocket-red business dress and jacket. Its simplicity, class and supreme comfort beat out the tough competition. She would announce the winner right after the fashion show.

Now they just had to execute everything they'd planned for the last three months to perfection. All that work and it came down to one night. It was crazy exciting and nerve-racking.

Michael had done an incredible job with the publicity and the guest list. The set designers and the contractors had decorated the runway and the venue to perfection, and the themed photo booths were generously sponsored by corporations, adding early heft to their fundraising efforts.

She was filled to the brim with anticipation, and tormented by dread. Adelaide would soon have no excuses left to hang on to Michael. She'd vowed to let him go without drama. With a smile and a friendly hug. He cared deeply for her—she knew that in her soul. It would break his heart to hurt her, and telling him she loved him would do exactly that because he would still leave her.

Michael wanted her like a man starved. That much was real. As real as the sky and the air they breathed. But desire was only desire. It wasn't love. He believed without question that whatever they had should end. But Adelaide was convinced it was because he was hiding something from her. The prospect of forever and the chance of hurting her had held him back from the beginning. If only the stubborn man would trust her with his secret, then they might have a chance for more.

Adelaide scratched out the figure she'd been drawing and crumpled the paper with pent-up frustration. She didn't want to risk hurting him by telling him she loved him, but losing him would break her soul. All of her. Michael was her everything, just as her mom had been everything to her dad. But what choice did she have?

She stopped breathing. Adelaide *did* have a choice.

She could fight for Michael. Unlike her dad, who had lost her mom to death. *I have the choice to fight for him. To fight for us.*

"Who's taking their portable sewing machines?" Chris asked the team.

"A couple of us are, so why don't you bring your MacGyver briefcase full of spools, pins and all that jazz," Mona shouted from across the studio.

"Done," said one of the designers with a quizzical look on her face. "What's MacGyver?"

"*Who* is Mac—oh, never mind." Mona shook her head.

All of her team members were at the studio, getting ready to go over to the loft together. They were having a full rehearsal run, and everyone tittered with anticipation and nerves.

"We're taking three cars, right?" Adelaide pushed herself to standing using her desk as support. She was low on battery. "Let's get a move on, guys."

The loft couldn't have turned out better. They'd kept the stark white walls and the exposed industrial ceiling, which were perfectly complemented by the floor-to-ceiling windows. To soften the space, they used warm fabrics and muted earthy colors to decorate throughout. Because they weren't relying on flashy lighting, they added crystals where they could to refract light. Adelaide's favorite was the curtain of tear-shaped crystals set against the deep blues and greens of a photo booth. And to avoid loud, pounding music and noise, they'd hired a baroque sextet to perform; the sound of their tuning filled the air at the rehearsal.

Adelaide was once again awed by what her design-

ers had accomplished in such a short time. Thanks to
them, she learned about different fabrics, materials and
their uses that she'd never dreamed of, and grown as
a designer.

Their fashion show consisted of three looks by each
designer. Business casual, business formal and evening wear. The business casual and formal collections
were amazing, combining cleaned-lined professionalism with as close to custom-fitted comfort as they
could get off the rack. But the evening wear excited
Adelaide the most.

French-seamed tuxes and suits with secret panels, as
well as the formal dresses, were to die for. The dresses
had bodices without a hint of textured embellishment
such as lace, sequins or glitter, which would irritate the
sensitive underarms of their target consumers. Instead,
her designers used creative methods of using painted
fabric, unique geometric shapes, and other too-many-
to-name techniques to embolden the bodice. It gave
Adelaide chills just thinking about them.

She had so much to be grateful for. By taking risks
and making herself vulnerable, her professional goal
was finally within reach. It was time she did the same
for her *real* life. For forever.

Michael let himself into the loft as quietly as he
could. The rehearsal was going full throttle, and there
wasn't a single noise in the space unless it was meant
to be made. Adelaide stood off to the side near the end
of the runway, whispering something into her headset.
The slight but constant movement of her head showed
that she was watching every detail and not missing a

thing. He was so proud of her, his shirt stretched taut across his puffed-out chest.

As he watched Adelaide in her element, conducting the dress rehearsal, reality slapped him in the face. This would all be over in three days. They would be over. The heart that had been singing with admiration and pride collapsed into itself. The sharp pain that ripped through him felt like being pierced through with a lance. The thought of losing her cut his soul in half.

He saw spots in front of him, and he forced himself to breath. Michael was in love with Adelaide. Madly, profoundly, desperately. Since when? It had happened so slowly, he didn't even realize it. Was it that night at the club when her dancing reduced him to a jealous caveman? Or even before then? When she returned home from college a confident, witty woman who could make him laugh with a single quip?

More than anything—he wanted to hold on to her. She was his and he never wanted to let her go. But that wasn't love. That was greed and selfishness. He wasn't even able to give her a child of her own—the family she deserved. And if she chose to stay with him, she might lose the family she had. Her dream of becoming a part of Hansol would be shattered. All that loss… She would grow to resent him someday. She would want her family and her dream back. In the end, she would leave him. Just as his ex-wife had.

His hands fisted at his sides, and his teeth bit into his cheeks. The thought of another man loving his Adelaide, making her laugh, making her fall apart, made him want to burn the world down. It almost made him not care if he deprived her of having her own family. Not care if he was being the ultimate selfish bastard. He would be the bastard who loved her more than the world. The bastard who worshipped the ground she walked on.

Michael couldn't be near her right now. He couldn't look at her or breathe the same air as her without snatching her away from there. Away from the world. He'd try to find a way to tie her to him. To somehow make her stay. But that wasn't love. He couldn't do that to her.

So he left.

He walked out of the loft and blindly drove himself to the Ritz. Garrett had him on his guest list to his old penthouse. It was the closet place he could think of for privacy. When he got himself to his best friend's place—the one he was badly tempted to betray by holding on to Adelaide—he threw his suit jacket and tie onto a couch and grabbed the fullest bottle of liquor there was at the bar.

And he proceeded to get himself properly drunk.

He didn't know how much time had passed, but darkness had settled around him. He was halfway through his bottle, and his head felt like it was filled with cotton, but his thoughts and desires were crystal clear. And loud. *Mine. Mine. Mine.*

*No. Not mine.* He loved her, and that meant he had to let her go. What brief happiness they might share wouldn't last as she dealt with losing her dream, losing her family and losing her chance to have a child of her own. With so much loss, how happy could they be? For how long? It was better this way. Michael couldn't give her everything she deserved, but he could give her freedom to find a man who could give her everything.

He took another swig from the bottle. The ding of

the elevator announced someone was in the penthouse. He dismissed it, thinking he'd probably imagined it.

"What the hell?" Adelaide's voice shook. He belatedly remembered she was also on Garrett's guest list. His eyes had adjusted to the dark and he could make out her expression with the help of the city lights outside. She looked absolutely livid. "What the literal hell, Michael?"

"Howdy, Adelaide," he said cheerily. Maybe he'd succeeded in the getting-drunk department. Or maybe he was afraid and was pretending he wasn't about to lose her. "It's great to see you."

"I've been texting you and calling you for hours. I even drove to your house. I broke in through your freaking kitchen door to make sure you were okay. But you weren't there," she shouted. Michael cringed as her voice shot painfully through his head. "I couldn't find you anywhere. Because you're here, getting shit-faced for some reason. Ignoring all my calls and worrying me sick. If I hadn't remembered you sometimes stayed here after working late, I wouldn't even be here. Again, what the hell is going on?"

"I'm sorry, baby. I had my phone off, and I didn't know how much time had passed," he said, truly sorry for worrying her. "I was at the rehearsal. Everything looked spectacular. But I had a hell of a day, and I didn't want my mood to taint everyone's high."

"You should've at least texted me," she said, her nostrils flaring slightly. Her anger was slowly seeping out of her stance.

"I know. I screwed up. I didn't want to worry you, and I only ended up worrying you more. Will you forgive me?" He stood from the couch and walked toward her. When he reached her and kissed her softly on the lips, she accepted his kiss. *My sweet, generous Adelaide.*

Her soft hand rose to cup his face. "Are you okay? What happened?"

"Oh, some people have their heads in the clouds and refuse to listen to reason. It makes my life difficult when someone hangs on to hope when there is none." He huffed a humorless laugh. "Foolish dreams."

"And you don't want to be the one to break it to them. I think I understand," she said. "But, hey. Don't beat yourself up about it. You have to do your job. You're doing what's best for them."

"Am I?"

"Of course. You would never intentionally hurt anyone."

Her goodness and her trust in him tore him to pieces. How could he not love this woman? With a quiet groan, he kissed her with all the pent-up love inside him. He kissed her and didn't bother to come up for air. For tonight. He wanted to make love to her like she was his. His forever.

With a sound between a whimper and a moan, Adelaide opened up wider for him and tangled her tongue with his. Her kiss was demanding and challenging. His hands roamed down her front and pulled her shirt out of her skirt. He began working on her buttons, but impatience roared in him. He grasped the two sides of her shirt and tore it off her, sending buttons flying all over the floor.

"Michael," she moaned, struggling with his shirt.

He cursed under his breath and took care of his shirt the same way. He wanted her naked skin against his. He was burning up from within, and he couldn't wait to have her. He led her to the couch and pulled her onto his lap, spreading her legs to straddle him. Michael roughly pushed up her skirt. He unbuckled his belt and pushed his pants and boxers down far enough to reach his aching erection. Pulling aside her panties, he whispered, "I need you now, baby. I promise you it'll be okay."

"It's okay. I'm on the pill. Take me now. I want nothing between us."

He ignored the irony of her words and surged inside her. "You'll be safe. I promise you."

"I know," she panted. "I know."

He licked her throat with a hard stroke of his tongue, then suckled her pretty, rock-hard nipples. She lurched into him and groaned throatily. She drove him crazy. The hot heat of her center cradled him, and he was home.

"You're mine." He tilted her hips and surged in deeper. "Say it, Adelaide."

"I'm yours, Michael. Yours forever."

"Mine. Forever."

"And you're mine, Michael. Forever."

"I'm yours," he said fervently.

They found an impossibly fast and hard tempo, her pounding down on him surge for surge, again and again until they came together with a sharp, passionate shout. His body spent and his mind painfully clear, he stood with Adelaide cradled in his arms.

He took them to the guest bedroom, and he eased her down onto the bed and climbed in after her. Tonight, they were going to spend the night together in each other's arms. For the first time. For the last time.

"I love you," he whispered into her hair, and fell asleep before she responded.

# Fourteen

Michael Reynolds loved her. He loved her! She'd heard him as clear as day before they fell asleep.

*I love you.*

Now she was awake and staring into the beautiful face of the man who loved her. The man she loved back most madly. And suddenly all her worries about him wanting to end things, and her having to go along with it because she didn't want him hurt, seemed a foolish waste of time.

But now that she knew, she was going to enjoy every second of the happiness she and Michael would share. Together. She couldn't stop herself from cradling his stubbled cheek in her hand. He was so beautiful. He stirred in his sleep so she brushed her lips across his.

"Good morning, Michael."

He smiled sleepily with his eyes still closed. The smile of a content man. She grinned back at him with her eyes shining. But then his eyes snapped open, the grin transforming into a frown.

"Morning, beautiful," he said, scrambling out of bed and picking up his clothes from the floor.

"Michael?"

"I shouldn't have kept you here last night," he said with regret written across his face as he hastily put on his clothes.

Was that all he had to say? Was he trying to gloss over the fact that he'd told her he loved her last night?

"*You* didn't keep me here. *I* chose to stay the night with you. Because I wanted to," she said, her concern turning into irritation.

"I'm going to leave now. You can leave in an hour or so. It's not much, but at least we won't run the risk of being photographed together."

"You can't leave now." She was at a disadvantage for this discussion, naked in bed while he was fully dressed. She wrapped the sheet around herself and got to her feet. "Not until we've talked."

"I have to. We'll talk later. I promise." He walked over to her and gently squeezed her shoulders. "But you wanted to keep our relationship a secret. We can't become careless two days before the event. Did you forget your grandmother's admonition?"

"Of course, I didn't forget. This fashion show's more important to me than to anyone else. But what we have to discuss is even more important."

"Your image has been rehabilitated and the charity event is poised for success. Having a picture of us walking out of the hotel together will be a disaster. We'll talk tonight."

"I thought you finally saw me as a grown woman who could make her own decisions. I don't need anyone—including you—to tell me what's best for me."

"Come on, Adelaide." He ran his hand through his already tousled hair. "You're not being fair. I'm trying to do my job."

"Fine. Do your job. But you can wait an hour, because I'll be leaving first. I have work to do."

She grabbed her crumpled clothes and got dressed in the bathroom. She was too furious to bother washing her hair, so she put it up in a loose knot at the top of her head. She buttoned her blazer, hoping it hid her lost shirt buttons sufficiently. When she came out, Michael was pacing the bedroom with worry written across his face.

"Adelaide," he said, coming toward her with his hand outstretched.

"Keep your hands off of me," she snapped, stepping out of his reach. The man had told her he loved her last night, and now he was pretending nothing happened. Her grandmother was important. Her dreams were important. But so was love. Love was very important.

"I know. I know what you want to talk about. But it has to wait. Right now we need to stop this catastrophe from happening, then we can talk," Michael said, a hint of desperation in his voice.

"What's half an hour going to change? We need to talk now."

"It's still early enough in the morning when not a lot of people would see us. We need to leave as soon as possible."

"Fine. I'm leaving."

"Not like that," Michael pleaded, jumping into the elevator with her. "Don't leave angry. I'm only doing this to protect you."

"Do me a favor, and don't," she snapped, and stepped out of the elevator when the doors opened in the lobby.

"Adelaide. You can't leave like this."

She kept walking and had stepped out through the exit when Michael gripped her arm. She jerked her arm free. "Why ever not?"

He didn't have a chance to respond before a handful of paparazzi surrounded them, snapping picture after picture.

After everything she'd accomplished, he'd done this to her. Two days before the event. He'd broken her heart, ruined her reputation and jeopardized her career. He'd done this.

He put his arm around her, tucking her head into his chest, and hurried her to his car. Quickly settling her into the passenger seat, Michael jumped into the driver's seat and drove away from the flashing cameras.

"Goddammit," he yelled, pounding his hand on the wheel. "I'm sorry, Adelaide. But I'll take care of it. I won't let anything harm you."

"Actually, I can take care of this on my own," she said in a cold, poised voice. "I have the interview with the morning show scheduled for tomorrow. I'll take a moment to defuse any rumors. Those pictures cannot affect the fashion show."

"But they could ambush you on live TV."

"I can handle it," she snapped. "You need to stop underestimating me."

"That's not—"

"I can't do this right now. Please take me home."

"Not the office?"

"And what? Are you going to face Grandmother on your own?" He shut his mouth. He couldn't believe he'd forgotten about Mrs. Song. She should've been on the top of his list for troubleshooting. He was so worried for Adelaide that he wasn't thinking straight, and that wasn't helping anyone, especially her. "Her schedule is open this morning, so she should be home."

"Okay. I'll take you home."

"It's nice to finally agree on something." She was fuming, and he couldn't blame her.

They drove to Pacific Palisades in stilted silence, and Michael's mind was spinning with how they would explain themselves to Mrs. Song.

"We need to figure out what we're telling your grandmother," he said, breaking the silence with a businesslike tone.

They couldn't let their emotion overtake them right now. They had to come up with a plausible explanation to convince Mrs. Song that Adelaide was dedicated to the fashion show and not up to her old ways. This morning shouldn't reflect negatively on the hard work she'd put in so far.

"We're telling her the truth," she said, still looking out the window.

"Excuse me?" He must've misheard her. They couldn't admit to breaking her trust. Not now.

"You heard me. Lying by omission is one thing, but I'm not going to lie to my grandmother's face."

"You can't do that. Think about what's at stake."

"I know exactly what's at stake. I never lost sight of it for a second. But with what happened, I have to own up to it and trust Grandmother to understand why we did what we did."

Michael gripped the steering wheel until his knuckles turned white. *Why we did what we did.* Why indeed? To satiate our physical needs? Hell, no. It was love. It was always love. But he couldn't admit that to Adelaide in front of Mrs. Song. He couldn't allow them to enter into a battle of wills over him. He wasn't worth it. He refused to allow this to happen just days before the fashion show.

Adelaide seemed to take his silence for acquiescence and didn't argue further, but Michael knew exactly what he had to do.

She let herself out of the car when he parked, and he followed her into the house. Liliana met them at the door, but her smile slid off her face as soon as she saw their expressions. "Mrs. Song is in the study."

"Thank you," Michael said quietly, and followed Adelaide down the hallway.

Adelaide knocked on the door without hesitation, determination etched into her face.

"Come in," Mrs. Song said from behind the door. When the two of them walked in, her eyes rounded ever so slightly. "What are you two doing here at this hour? I trust there are no problems with the fashion show."

"No, there are no problems with the show. We came because we have something to tell you. Michael and

I've been seeing each other," Adelaide said without pre-amble.

When she took a breath to continue, Michael cut in. "But it's over now. Spending so much time together the last few months brought up some emotions we mistook for love. We're past it and have been fully focused on the fashion show."

Adelaide gazed at him with heartbreak in her eyes. *Damn it.* Her look tore him with guilt and regret like physical pain. But he couldn't stop now. He had to be strong for both of them.

"What is this all about?" Mrs. Song said with quiet command. It was clear she expected them to tell her everything this instant.

"We were seen coming out of Garrett's penthouse this morning, and there are going to be pictures," Adelaide said boldly.

"We were working on last-minute preparations for the event," he interrupted once more. "But the media is going to try to spin it into something entirely different."

"You two were careless enough to let this happen two days before the fashion show?" Mrs. Song demanded, her voice rising.

"Call it last-minute nerves. Preoccupation with D-Day." He kept his tone even and professional. After all, this was a business discussion. "Whatever the reason, we made a mistake, but we will fix the situation, Mrs. Song."

"Is this true, Adelaide?"

"Yes, *Hal-muh-nee.* We made a mistake," she said to avoid lying outright to her grandmother, and glared at him with eyes filled with resentment. He'd pushed her into a corner, smothering her efforts to tell the truth. Her shoulders dropped imperceptibly, but her disappointment was palpable. Michael felt a fissure opening up in the center of his heart. "I'm going to handle this situation, and pull off the fashion show without a hitch. I won't disappoint you."

"This is not the time for arguments or division in our family. What happened has happened. I trust you to correct the situation," Mrs. Song said, to Adelaide and Michael's shock. "You can do this. You must do this. Your position at Hansol still depends on the success of the fashion show. I won't be an obstacle in your way, but I'm not holding your hand through this. You are a Song. Show me what you're made of."

*Thank God. Adelaide still has a chance. Her dream is alive and well.* But the cracks in his heart still grew and spread to the outer edges. It was a miracle it didn't crumble all together.

"I'm sorry about this mess, but nothing is going to derail the show," Adelaide said with absolute conviction. "Your trust in me won't be misplaced, Grandmother."

But Michael knew Adelaide's trust in him was destroyed for good.

# Fifteen

"Michael and I are old friends. Actually, we're closer to family than friends. We don't do it as often as before, but we sometimes fight like siblings do. That's all that scene was in front of the Ritz. We were both exhausted from the fashion show rehearsal—which was amazing. The tickets for the event are sold out, but we'll be streaming live and allowing viewers to bid online in an auction for some of the designs." Adelaide clapped her hands over her chest to show her enthusiasm for the television audience. She was indeed excited about the event. It was just that she had a gaping hole where her heart used to be, and she had to lay it on thick to cover how dead she felt inside. "But what was I talking about? Oh, of course. My fight with Michael. Long story short we had a disagreement over something, and it blew into the biggest fight we've ever had."

"Would you call it a lovers' spat?" the morning show host asked with a teasing grin.

"There's no love lost between us. I'll tell you that much." She gave the host an exaggerated wink. "I'm so embarrassed at how immature that sounds, but lack of sleep and stress can make a person do some silly stuff. Once we pull off the best damn fashion show and auction tomorrow, I'm sure we'll go back to being easy friends."

"The air practically crackles when you talk about the fashion show. Could you give us your best pitch before we go to commercial?"

"This world is beautiful because of its diversity. This fashion show will celebrate those differences. My greatest hope is for the event to illustrate that acceptance of all diversity showcases the best of humanity."

The cameras cut out to a round of applause, and Adelaide was able to leave the studio with a triumphant smile on her face. Her personal life might've been a wreck, but she was a Song and she wouldn't let anything, even a broken heart, interfere with the charity event and the cause so worthy of her and the designers' efforts.

While she'd thought all the hard work was done, the last-minute preparations kept her up all night. Not that she would've been able to sleep otherwise. Every cell in her body hurt. Breathing hurt. Existing hurt. Working didn't ease the pain, but it distracted her from the most painful thing of all: reliving her argument with Michael. Hearing his words on a loop.

*Emotions we mistook for love... We're past it...*

She knew it wasn't true, and that was what hurt her the most. He didn't trust her with his love. With his heart. He thought she would crumble and fall at the first sign of hardship, and he was afraid of holding her up for the rest of their life. A burden he had to carry, along with the secret he held so tightly to himself.

The rest of the day rushed by with Adelaide packing extra supplies just in case. When she bought ten rolls of duct tape thinking it would come in handy, Adelaide accepted that she was panicking. And she wasn't the only one. Her anxious designers texted her with last minute questions until her cell phone overheated.

Before she could properly absorb what was happening, it was time for the fashion show to begin. Adelaide wore an edgy white tux sans tie that she'd designed as her contribution to the collection. It fit so well and allowed such great range of movement that she almost forgot she was in formal wear.

Michael came, but he stayed away from her except to say hello and wish her luck. Perhaps, it was for the best. She wouldn't have been able to concentrate on the proceedings 100 percent with him so near. Soon the cocktail reception came to a close, and she escorted her grandmother and the VIPs to their seats, adrenaline coursing through her veins. *This is it.*

The models showcased the immaculate business attires to the *oohs* and *aahs* of the guests. But when they walked the runway in the formal suits and dresses, there was only hushed awe.

Their guests were entranced by the setting, the music and, most of all, the clothes. From everyday business wear to evening wear, these were clothes that people with autism could wear with confidence—without the discomfort that would've prevented them from looking and performing their best. Adelaide was so proud of her designers and what they had accomplished.

Adelaide swallowed the emotion clogging her throat, and took the stage to introduce her amazing design team to the pounding applause of their guests.

"May I have your attention please," Adelaide said into the mic. "It's time to announce the winner of the design contest. As you guys can guess, it was a tight race. But this designer's work captured the very spirit of this fashion show. And the winner is… Mona Andrews!"

The applause rang like thunder and her entire design team jumped to their feet shouting and congratulating Mona, who cried happy tears. Adelaide couldn't have wished for a better outcome.

The auction was a spirited and exciting affair with the guests competing for their favorite pieces. The bid for Mona's award-winning red suit was cutthroat. Adelaide watched the proceedings come to an end, feeling weightless with elation. They'd done it. She'd done it.

Her design team rushed to her and enveloped her in a group hug. They were a happy, whooping mess of entangled limbs.

"You guys were so amazing, and I'm so proud of you," she said, untangling herself.

"We had an amazing leader," Chris said, and the others echoed his sentiment.

"Go and have fun now. You deserve it." She sent off the design students with more hugs and congratulations.

"Adelaide." Her grandmother materialized at her side and pulled her into a tight hug. "Congratulations, my heart. I'm so proud of you."

"Oh, God. Thank you, Hal-muh-nee." Tears sprang to her eyes.

"The woman who pulled this spectacular event off... that is you. Never doubt who you are. Never doubt what you're capable of achieving," Grandmother said with a catch in her voice. "You're going to be an amazing department head."

Adelaide was rendered speechless for a moment, and it felt as though her heart had skipped several beats. When she regained her ability to breathe and speak, she gripped her grandmother's hands in her own trembling ones and said, "I won't let you down, Hal-muh-nee."

"I know you won't." Tears glistened in her grandmother's eyes.

"Congratulations, cuz." Colin wrapped her up in a bear hug.

"Thank you, Colin," Adelaide said hugging him back.

"Enjoy the moment," he said. "Hal-muh-nee, may I escort you to your car?"

"Yes, I should be on my way." Her grandmother squeezed Adelaide's hand one more time before being led away by Colin.

Adelaide stayed until the last of the guests and staff left. Except for Michael. He stood quietly in shadow against a wall following her with his eyes. Adelaide locked the loft door and turned to face him from across the room.

"Are you finally ready to talk?" she asked in a deceptively calm tone. Inside, she was trembling with fear—afraid of what was to come, the success of the night fading into the background. "What you said to my grandmother, and what I said on the show... Is that what you really want?"

"Adelaide." Her name was a plea on his lips. *But a plea for what?* He pushed himself off the wall and drew closer to her. In the light, she could see the pallor of his skin, his drawn and tired expression. "That's what we agreed to from the beginning. It's for the best."

"Despite what I said, we don't need to end things." She breathed in and out several times to keep her voice—and panic—from rising. "It's not that my reputation is suddenly unimportant to me, but being with you won't harm me. There might be talk in the beginning, but soon they would see that I'm a grown woman in a committed relationship. It's mature, grown-up and boring. They'll forget about us in no time."

"It's not only the public. What about your grandmother? The show was a huge success tonight. No one could question that. You are going to get that department head position at Hansol. If you oppose your grandmother now, all that could be jeopardized."

"We're not talking about a casual affair. Why would Grandmother disapprove of us? You're just grasping at straws to end this relationship."

"There are things you don't understand, but I won't come between your family and your dream. This has to end now."

"But that night...you told me you loved me." She held her breath, praying he wouldn't deny it.

"I know," he said simply.

"Then why? Michael, I love you, too. I've always loved you."

"No. You can't." He stumbled back, then widened his stance and steadied himself. "I know you had a crush on me when you were a little girl, but that wasn't love. Even if it was, you're just confusing the past with the present. The passion we share is extraordinary, but it isn't love. Please. You can't love me."

"Why can't I love you, Michael?" She took hesitant steps toward him. He retreated before he stopped himself. "Why can't we be together?"

"Trust me. We can't be together. You can't love me."

"Why do you keep saying that?" She reached him at last and put her hand over his heart. "Let me love you. I don't need anything from you. If what we have is all you could give me, then it'll have to be enough. Just don't push away my love, Michael. It has always been and will always be yours. You deserve to be loved. Let me be the one to do it."

His eyes grew impossibly wide, and his breathing grew shallow and rapid. Then he shut his eyes and opened lifeless eyes to her. "It's over, Adelaide."

"No, Michael. Please."

"If you stay with me, you'll lose everything that matters to you."

"What are you hiding? Please tell me. We can figure this out together."

"You don't want to be with me." He took a shuddering breath. "I don't want to be with you."

"You're a horrible liar, Michael Reynolds."

"Adelaide, I—"

"That's enough. I hear you loud and clear. I don't

know what you're hiding. Or why you're so afraid. But I hear you." Adelaide took a step away from him, then another. "You just broke us. Not this relationship or our hearts. But us. You and I will never be the same again. Whatever you're hiding from—whatever you're protecting yourself from—I hope it's worth it."

She'd had enough; his lies were hurting him as much as they were hurting her. And there was the one truth that had never changed. He might've loved her, but he didn't trust her. She was still a helpless little girl to him. A burden. Not a partner. Never a partner.

Her soul exhaled a weary sigh and lay down on the cold ruins of her heart, and Adelaide left without a backward glance. Without tears.

The next morning, Adelaide didn't bother getting out of bed. The fashion show was done, and her design team was probably packing their things from the studio and saying goodbyes. Adelaide's goodbyes would have to wait. She deserved a day to wallow in her suffering.

The intense pain had faded now into a dull ache, and she could live with that. It seemed as though that was something she would have to live with for the rest of her life. She'd lost Michael, but she would get Hansol. The fashion show couldn't have been a bigger success. She had accomplished what she'd set out to do. Like Grandmother, she would devote her life to Hansol and somehow fill the void inside her.

Adelaide stared up at the ceiling. It was white. She was glad she'd kept it white, while she had the rest of her bedroom painted a light jade green. The emptiness of the white ceiling felt familiar and undemanding, and it calmed her.

Liliana walked into her room after a soft knock. She bore a cup of milk and a slice of toast. The softness of her gaze, the concern in her expression, were a lot harder to look at than the ceiling. Much harder.

"Adelaide, dear. Mrs. Song wishes to see you. Do you think you could eat a few bites of this and head down?"

"No, thank you."

"I'm so sorry, but I can't leave your room until you do." She sighed quietly and sat on the edge of her bed. "We know something happened a couple days ago. You've been dragging yourself around like a ghost. It's a wonder how well you held yourself together for the fashion show."

"It just hurts."

"Oh, my dear." Liliana squeezed her hand gently. "Maybe your grandmother can help. She has experience in how to put one step in front of another until the pain becomes bearable."

"Okay, but no food."

"All right. Let me help you."

The room spun when she stood, but Liliana wrapped her arm around her shoulder as she guided her down the stairs to Grandmother's room. With each step, Adelaide found the strength to stand on her own. By the time she was at her grandmother's door, she felt strong. And furious.

She pushed open the door without a knock and kneeled on the *bang-suk*. The floor mat felt like blocks of wood against her knees this morning.

"You summoned me, Grandmother?"

"Adelaide, look at me."

She raised her eyes, and let all her resentment and anger spill out through them. "Are you disappointed in me for taking the day off, *Hal-muh-nee*? Should I be sitting in my studio, waiting for my department to be formed?"

*"Ah-ga."*

"Stop. Not now. I am not your baby. I am a grown woman. Can you ever accept that?"

She was being unimaginably rude to her elder for no good reason. *Why* did Adelaide feel so angry with her grandmother? Why did she want to lash out at her?

"I haven't been keeping you out of Hansol because I thought you wouldn't be able to handle it. It was because I knew you would do only too well. You and I are so much alike. That's what made me afraid. I chose to dedicate myself to Hansol when your grandfather died, and I neglected every other aspect of my life. Even you children."

"No, that's not—"

"Listen, child. I let my ambition blind me, but the company wasn't enough to make me whole. I needed my children and grandchildren. Our family. Each and every one of you matter more than the world. But I nearly lost sight of that, and trapped myself in a lonely cell of my creation." Her grandmother reached for Adelaide's hand. "I didn't want that for you. I couldn't want that for you. I thought if I dissuaded you from working at the company, you would find your own life. Pursue your own dream. But now I know—Hansol is your dream. Besides, you're stronger than me. You would use that clever brain of yours to figure out how to balance your life. I am so proud of the woman you've become."

"Oh, *Hal-muh-nee*. All this time, I believed you didn't think I was good enough."

"I know. I know, *ah-ga*, and I'm so sorry for trying to relive my life through yours."

"I… I have something to tell you. I'm in love with Michael, but he left me, and it hurts more than I can bear." Adelaide laid her head on her grandmother's leg, curling up on the floor. "He doesn't see me for the woman I've become, but as a burden. He loves me and I love him more than life, but he doesn't trust me with his heart."

"I suspected," she spoke under her breath, "but I didn't know it had come so far."

"I'm sorry I kept it from you. I stupidly thought I could let him go when the time came, but I couldn't. I tried to hang on to him…"

"Oh, my sweet child. He sees you and loves you as much as a man could ever love a woman." She smoothed her hand over Adelaide's bent head. "Don't give up on him."

"It's too late, because he's given up on me. He's given up on us." Adelaide took a deep breath and raised herself into a sitting position. "I can't be near him. I'm eager to do my part for Hansol, but please send me to New York. I could start my clothing line there. I can't be here right now."

"That isn't difficult to arrange, but are you sure?"

"That is the only thing I'm sure of. I need to leave and move past this. I can't let it destroy me. My new position will help me get through this. I'll survive, *Hal-muh-nee*, but not here. Not like this."

"Whatever you need, I will make happen. Remember, I am always here for you."

Michael didn't remember driving home from the fashion show, but he was inside his house. Everything looked different—drab and colorless—in the weak morning light. In fact, his house looked downright ugly. He hated it. He hated everything: Himself, most of all.

Michael glanced at the half-empty bottle of Scotch on the coffee table. He remembered now. He'd poured himself endless shots of the stuff and must've fallen asleep on the couch. Now morning was here, and he'd neglected his duties. The fashion show was an enormous success, but he should've been monitoring for unscrupulous bottom-feeders trying to taint Adelaide's success with rumors about their night at the Ritz.

Belatedly, he picked up his phone and scrolled through his alerts. Autism awareness was still a trending topic among many of the influential attendees, including Mateo Sanchez and his daughter. And, luckily for him, the tabloids and gossip columns were otherwise occupied.

Michael laid his head back on the couch and covered his eyes with his hand. Where was Adelaide? How was she doing? Was she hurting as much as he was? God, he couldn't bear to think that. He didn't know losing her would hurt this much. As though his heart was torn out of him.

He'd hurt Adelaide to protect her in the only way he knew, but he needed to see her. Michael had no idea what he would say or do, but he had to see with his own eyes that she was okay. Or as okay as she could be after what he'd done to her. What could he do to ease her pain? He called her, but she'd blocked him on her cell. He called her office, but she didn't pick up there, either. When he reached the receptionist, he was informed she wasn't in.

Then she must be home. After a quick shower, he jumped in his fastest sports car. His heart bruising his rib cage, Michael broke every speed limit on his way to her house.

"Liliana, I need to see Adelaide," he said as soon as the front door of the Song residence cracked open.

"Michael," she said rather coldly. Then she continued with utmost politeness, "Why don't you come in and I'll let Mrs. Song know that you're here. I have a feeling she might want to speak with you."

"But Adelaide—"

"Don't push your luck with me. I have never seen that dear child suffer so much." She choked on a sob. "I don't care what you did or why. Do not demand anything from me, because it's all I can do not to slam the door in your face right now."

That was enough to rob Michael of speech. The unflappable, mild-mannered Liliana was nowhere to be seen. To think he'd caused this change in her spoke volumes as to what state Adelaide was in. *Oh, God. What have I done?*

He followed her to the door of Mrs. Song's room without another word, and stood still while she went inside to speak with the family matriarch. When she came out, she shot him another furious glance, as though she couldn't bear even to look at his sorry mug.

"She'll see you."

"Thank you, Liliana."

With a huff, she turned her back on him and disappeared down the hall. He entered Mrs. Song's room and knelt on the *bang-suk*. "Good morning, Mrs. Song."

"It's well past noon and it isn't a particularly good afternoon," she replied stoically.

"You might not think I deserve to, but I need to see Adelaide. I just want to make sure she's okay."

"No, you don't deserve to see my granddaughter. And no, she is far from okay."

"I'm so sorry." He gulped down the lump in his throat. "Please, Mrs. Song. Could I see Adelaide even if it's for the last time?"

She sighed, her iron mask softening as she looked closely at him. "What have you been doing to yourself?"

"It doesn't matter. I broke her heart, and I let her down in the worst possible way. If I thought I didn't deserve her before, this certainly confirms it. But still… I need to see her."

"She's already gone, Michael."

Cold sweat broke out on his forehead. *No.* "Gone? Gone where?"

"She left for the airport half-an-hour ago to be with Garrett and Natalie. When she feels ready, she will work at the New York branch."

"Was she so angry with me that she wanted to put the entire country between us?" He should be grateful that she hadn't disappeared to another continent. Even he wished he could flee from himself, because being in his skin was nauseating.

"I don't think she has room for anger in her devastation. The Song family's biggest strength and weakness is that we love too deeply," Grace Song said, looking out the window. "She loved you with all her heart, Michael. She wanted to be everything for you. When you pushed her away, she took that as her failure. She thinks she failed you, because she wasn't good enough for you."

"Her not good enough for me? You know I can't give her children. Even if I was whole, I wouldn't have deserved her. She is the most amazing woman I know."

"She believes that you don't trust her with your love. That you still see her as a helpless child. A burden." His breath caught in his throat, and his eyes bugged with shock. *A burden?* But before he could utter a word, Mrs. Song continued, "Have you even tried telling her that you can't have children? Did you ever think that it should be her choice to decide whether she wanted to stay with you or not? Do you even know if she wants children? If she'd want to adopt?"

"No, but it's more than that." He lifted his eyes to meet hers. "I didn't believe you would allow Adelaide to marry me. You and James want her to have children of her own. I don't blame you, but I couldn't make Adelaide choose between me and her family. If she lost your support now, what would happen to her dream of joining Hansol?"

"*Allow* her to marry you? Hasn't Garrett taught you anything? Us Songs are relentless when it comes to the people we love. I wouldn't be able to stop Adelaide from choosing you even if I wanted to. And that brings us to the next point. How dare you assume I would hold your infertility against you? And how dare you assume I would be so unfair and unreasonable as to keep Adelaide out of Hansol after all she has accomplished?"

Michael felt the walls crashing in around him, and the sound of the truth rendered him temporarily mute. *It was you.* All this time, he had told himself it was Adelaide and Mrs. Song who stood in the way of their forever. But it had been him all along. He was afraid Adelaide would grow to resent him and leave him. Like Kathy had done. He couldn't bear the thought of losing her, so he had chosen when and how they would end. When they didn't have to end at all.

"Mrs. Song, I never believed you to be any of those things. Now I know that."

"You were so entrenched in your own shame and guilt that you treated the woman you love like a thoughtless child."

"I was wrong. So very wrong." He had ruined the best thing in his life because of his fear and insecurities. "Do you think she'll listen to me now? Am I too late?"

"How would I know that, child? What I've told you, I only know because she told me as she sobbed in my arms. I almost despised you in that moment. Do you know that?" He watched incredulously as the formidable Grace Song teared up in front of him. *God, what have I done?* "I've never seen my baby hurt so much. A part of her shattered, and it killed me to watch."

"Please give me a chance to make it up to her, and to you," Michael begged helplessly.

"If you weren't like one of my own, I would banish you from my sight. But it's too late for that. You've been

mine for a long time now. If I could, I would still hide
Adelaide from you, but you are hers to take or leave.
She is her own person and it's her decision. Not yours,
and certainly not mine." She took a deep breath and all
signs of her prior vulnerability disappeared. "When you
fight for her, you must fight with everything in you.
Because both of you deserve to know once and for all
whether you are worthy of her."

# Sixteen

"Are you sure there isn't anything else I can get for you?" Natalie asked, tucking a blanket around Adelaide's shoulders.

"I need you to stop fussing over me, preggers," she said with a mock frown. "If you tire yourself out because of me, I'm checking myself into a hotel."

Her sister-in-law gasped theatrically. "You would bring shame upon our family by leaving? We'll be forever known as the heartless Korean-Americans who let their own sister sleep in a hotel."

Adelaide laughed. It sounded hollow because of the gaping whole inside her, but it was genuine. Having Garrett, Natalie and Sophie around her made her as happy as she could be at the moment. She was lucky to have such great family. And being with her New York family felt a bit more freeing than being back in LA with her grandmother and dad.

But that didn't mean she would let them coddle her. Adelaide planned on searching for her own place as soon as she secured a Realtor. She hadn't come to New York to wallow like a jilted woman. She'd come to move on from her heartbreak, and focus on starting her new line at Hansol. If she kept moving, she wouldn't have a chance to fall prey to her sorrow.

"Are you sure you don't need anything else?" Garrett poked his head into the family room, holding on to Sophie's hand. The little girl grinned at her without a care in the world, and Adelaide loved her for it.

"Would both of you stop it now? I mean it. The last thing I need is to feel like a burden to you guys, too. Stop fussing. Now."

"Okay, okay. Jeez, sis. You're pretty scary when you put your foot down." Her big brother grinned. She couldn't help but notice how much he'd changed since he married Natalie, and felt a twinge of envy at their happiness. Which was small and ridiculous of her. Her own misery was just shadowing her thoughts. It wasn't the real her.

As they settled into playing with Sophie, the door buzzer rang. Everyone in the room stilled. It could be anyone. Maybe someone delivering a package. When the buzzer rang again, and then again, becoming urgent, Garrett looked out the window to the front entrance of their brownstone.

"What the ever-loving hell?" he muttered under his

breath, then shot a guilty glance at his daughter, who thankfully didn't seem to have heard. "It's Mike."

Adelaide sucked in a sharp breath. Whatever Natalie saw on Adelaide's face must've been alarming because she pulled her into her arms and started rocking her on the sofa.

"It's okay, love. You're safe. Garrett will send him on his way."

She couldn't answer so she let herself sink into her sister-in-law's embrace and closed her eyes tight, as though that might stop the buzzing. She was ready to move on. Truly she was. But that didn't mean she was ready to face Michael right this minute. Adelaide was strong, but she wasn't a masochist.

Leaving Sophie in her mother's care, Garrett stomped down the stairs like a giant in the clouds. The thump, thump, thump sounded so ominous that Adelaide felt a flash of fear for Michael. But before she could consider going downstairs, the door opened, then slammed shut after only a moment. She didn't hear Michael's voice, which she'd unconsciously been straining to hear. In fact, she didn't hear a single word exchanged between the two men.

When Garrett came back upstairs, Natalie rushed to him. He was flexing his wrist and wincing, and his wife cradled his hand and blew on his bruised knuckles.

"Did you hurt him?" Natalie sounded quite vicious. Adelaide could almost imagine the wreck she must seem for her sweet sister-in-law to become so furious.

Her brother responded with an equally vicious smile, "Hell, yeah."

*Oh, God.* Her overprotective brother had broken Michael's nose or jaw or something. Adelaide shot to her feet, ready to run downstairs. But she caught herself. What the hell was she doing? He had broken her heart twice over, and made it abundantly clear that there was no "us" for them. Going to him now would only result in more heartache.

"Adelaide!" Michael shouted from the street.

What was he doing?

"Adelaide, please. Let me see you. I just want to see that you're okay. Let me beg for your forgiveness and explain everything. If you still want to send me away, then I'll leave. I'll do everything you want me to do. Just let me see you."

She curled herself into a ball on the sofa and scrunched her eyes shut. *Don't listen to him. He'll hurt you.*

"I love you, Adelaide. So much. Please."

Adelaide's eyes shot open, and the fury on Garrett and Natalie's faces turned into shock.

"I think I fell in love with you that night at the club. You were so beautiful, and I wanted you to be mine." His voice broke on the word "mine," but he continued shouting, "And you could've been mine but I messed everything up so badly. I love you. Please just give me a chance to talk to you. Just this once. And if you still want me to leave, I will never bother you again."

*Oh, Michael. What are you doing to me?*

"Oh, my God." Adelaide gasped. "Are you bleeding?"

He might've been. He could taste iron in his mouth, and by the stinging in the corner of his lip, it was probably split and bleeding. But he didn't give a damn. All Michael cared about was that the front door had opened to reveal the most beautiful vision he could've dreamed of. She looked pale and drawn, but it was his Adelaide standing in the doorway.

Her hand rose to his face, but she dropped it to her side before she touched him. Michael's heart lurched painfully, but what had he expected? For her to welcome him with open arms? He would be even a bigger bastard if he expected to win her back so easily. He would beg and crawl, and fight for her forgiveness. He would give his everything to have her back.

Adelaide refusing him wasn't an option. Despite what he'd shouted up at her, he couldn't imagine giving up on her and walking out of her life. Ever. He would kneel outside Garrett's home until he became a pillar of sand if that was what it took. He would win her back or die trying.

"It's nothing, baby. I'm okay." Gingerly he took a step toward her, and sighed in relief when she didn't step back and slam the door.

"I'm not your baby. I'm not your anything anymore, Mike."

He flinched at her words, but he deserved it. "Please don't say that. At least not yet. I love you, Adelaide."

"You love me? You should make up your freaking mind." She paused and bit down on her lower lip, fighting the tears that welled up in her eyes. "Besides, your love means nothing without trust. You want me, but you won't have me because I'm a burden to you."

"No. God, no. You're not a burden. You were never a burden."

"Lies and more lies. You said you loved me, then pushed me away. You don't love me. That's why you can't trust me."

"I pushed you away because I thought it was the only way to protect you. When you told me you loved me, there was nothing I wanted more than to hold on to you. To keep you by my side forever. But I thought I was being selfish, because I'm broken and I don't deserve you. I told myself I wanted you to be with someone better than me. But please never doubt that I love you. You're my soul, my life. You deserve the world and more—only I can't give you that."

Confusion entered her eyes, but her expression remained cold and withdrawn. Michael raked shaking fingers through his hair. Cocking her head to the side, Adelaide studied him from head to toe, then sighed.

"You don't look well. Come inside. I don't want you to collapse on the doorstep."

In a daze, he followed Adelaide into the town house. Garrett looked down at him from the staircase, poised to throw another punch. If Michael's instincts hadn't kicked in, making him swerve to the side at the last minute, Garrett might have broken his nose or worse. But he didn't blame his friend. He deserved to have his ass kicked, and next time, he wouldn't move out of the way of his punch.

"Garrett and I are going to put Sophie to bed. You and Michael can use the family room in private," Natalie said quietly, dragging her reluctant husband away from the stairs.

Adelaide walked into the family room and perched on the ledge of the window. Then she waved her hand toward the sofa, reminding him to keep his distance. He obliged and took a seat at the far end of the couch.

"I don't understand," she said under her breath after a nerve-racking stretch of time. "What do you mean you're broken?"

"I can't give you children, Adelaide. I'm infertile." When she gasped softly, Michael continued, "I found out when Kathy and I were trying to start a family. All I ever wanted was a big family of my own. That's why I married someone I barely knew when she and I were both so young. When we found out I was infertile, Kathy was devastated. She grew increasingly resentful and distant until she finally left me."

"Michael, I'm so sorry you can't have children, and it's heartbreaking and infuriating that your ex-wife left you because of it. I understand your wound runs deep." She stood up from her perch. "But if you're telling me you crushed my heart to 'protect' me from your infertility, then maybe you're right. Maybe you don't deserve me."

"Adelaide…" The last flicker of hope began to fade inside him.

"You didn't even give me a chance to decide for myself. You just assumed I would be too weak to fight for us." Her voice began rising. "How could you think that I would rather leave you than stay with you and find a solution? Did you think I was looking for a freaking stud horse rather than a lifelong companion and partner?"

"I told myself that it would be selfish to hold on to you. I convinced myself that letting you go was the only way for me to love you." He was trembling from head to toe.

"You're a far bigger idiot than I ever gave you credit for."

"But that wasn't the truth at all. You see, I've been lying to myself all along. More than anything, I was afraid you wouldn't want me. I was so scared you would leave me that I held myself back."

"Goddammit, Michael." She covered her mouth as a sob escaped her. A flash of hope flared to life inside him. She'd called him "Michael." Did that mean a part of her still thought of him as hers? "If I thought you wanted me—if there was even the slightest chance that you wanted me to stay—I would've chosen you above all else. But you broke my heart and convinced me you couldn't trust me with yours."

"I know, and I'm going to have to with live with the fact I caused you pain for the rest of my life. But I love you, and trust you with my heart and scarred soul." It tore him apart that he'd hurt her, but it would be nothing compared to losing her forever. "I lost you because I let my shame and fear rule me, but never again. If you'll have me, I'll spend the rest of my life loving you with everything in me. Please tell me you'll give me a chance to make it up to you. To make you happy."

"What am I going to do with you?" She rushed to the sofa and gathered him in her arms. "I've always loved you and always will. I would never leave you if

I had my way. If you truly love me and *trust* me, then I'm yours forever."

"I love you and trust you with my life."

"Then you're mine now, Michael Reynolds."

"And you'll be mine?" Life burst through his veins again, and his love for her filled him with hope and strength.

"I've always been yours," she said without hesitation.

"Adelaide." And now there was only one thing he wanted—needed—with everything in him. Even if it was too soon. "Will you marry me?"

A blinding smile spread across her lovely face and tears filled her eyes. Eyes full of love. For him. Unable to hold back a second longer, Michael cradled her face between his hands and kissed her with all the love in his heart.

"Please make me the luckiest bastard on earth and marry me."

"I'll marry you, Michael," she said, tears flowing down her cheeks. "And you'll be mine forever."

"I couldn't exist any other way," he whispered.

Adelaide kissed him again and again until Michael finally believed it was all real.

\* \* \* \* \*

*If you loved
Michael and Adelaide's story,
don't miss*

Off Limits Attraction
*by Jayci Lee,*

*the next story in
The Heirs of Hansol series.*

*Available December 2020
exclusively
from Harlequin Desire.*

**WE HOPE YOU ENJOYED
THIS BOOK FROM**

# ♦ HARLEQUIN
# DESIRE

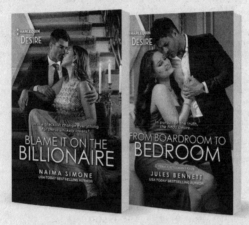

*Luxury, scandal, desire—welcome to
the lives of the American elite.*

Be transported to the worlds of oil barons, family dynasties,
moguls and celebrities. Get ready for juicy plot twists,
delicious sensuality and intriguing scandal.

**6 NEW BOOKS AVAILABLE EVERY MONTH!**

HDHALO2020

### #2761 BILLIONAIRE BEHIND THE MASK
*Texas Cattleman's Club: Rags to Riches*
by Andrea Laurence
A Cinderella makeover for busy chef Lauren Roberts leads to an unforgettable night of passion with a masked stranger—commanding CEO Sutton Wingate. But when the masks come off and startling truths are revealed, can these two find happily-ever-after?

### #2762 UNTAMED PASSION
*Dynasties: Seven Sins* • by Cat Schield
After one mind-blowing night together, bad boy photographer Oliver Lowell never expected to see Sammi Guzman again. Now she's pregnant. Passion has never been their problem, but can this black sheep tame his demons for a future together?

### #2763 TEMPTATION AT CHRISTMAS
by Maureen Child
Their divorce papers were never filed! So, Mia Harper tracks down her still-husband, Sam Buchanan, aboard his luxury cruise liner. Two weeks at sea tempts them into a hot holiday affair...or will it become something more?

### #2764 HIGH SOCIETY SECRETS
*The Sterling Wives* • by Karen Booth
Star architect Clay Morgan knows betrayal. Now he keeps his feelings—and beautiful women—at bay. Until he meets his new office manager, Astrid Sterling. Their sizzling chemistry is undeniable, but will a secret from her past destroy everything they've built?

### #2765 THE DEVIL'S BARGAIN
*Bad Billionaires* • by Kira Sinclair
The last person Genevieve Reilly should want is charming jewelry thief Finn DeLuca—even though he's the father of her son. But desire still draws her to him. And when old enemies resurface, maybe Finn is exactly the kind of bad billionaire she needs...

### #2766 AFTER HOURS REDEMPTION
*404 Sound* • by Kianna Alexander
A tempting new music venture reunites songwriter Eden Voss with her ex-boyfriend record-label executive Blaine Woodson. He wronged her in the past, so they vow to keep things strictly business this time. But there is nothing professional about the heat still between them...

**YOU CAN FIND MORE INFORMATION ON UPCOMING HARLEQUIN TITLES, FREE EXCERPTS AND MORE AT HARLEQUIN.COM.**

HDCNM0920

SPECIAL EXCERPT FROM

⟨H⟩**HARLEQUIN**

# DESIRE

*A tempting new music venture reunites songwriter
Eden Voss with ex-boyfriend Blaine Woodson, a record
label executive. He wronged her in the past, so they vow
to keep things strictly business this time. But there is
nothing professional about the heat still between them…*

*Read on for a sneak peek at*
After Hours Redemption *by Kianna Alexander.*

Singing through the opening verse, she could feel the smile
coming over her face. Singing gave her a special kind of joy, a
feeling she didn't get from anything else. There was nothing quite
like opening her mouth and letting her voice soar.

She was rounding the second chorus when she noticed Blaine
standing in the open door to the booth. Surprised, and a bit
embarrassed, she stopped midnote.

His face filled with earnest admiration, he spoke into the
awkward silence. "Please, Eden. Don't stop."

Heat flared in her chest, and she could feel it rising into her
cheeks. "Blaine, I…"

"It's been so long since I've heard you sing." He took a step
closer. "I don't want it to be over yet."

Swallowing her nervousness, she picked up where she'd left
off. Now that he was in the room, the lyrics, about a secret romance
between two people with plenty of baggage, suddenly seemed
much more potent.

And personal.

Suddenly, this song, which she often sang in the shower or
while driving, simply because she found it catchy, became almost
autobiographical. Under the intense, watchful gaze of the man
she'd once loved, every word took on new meaning.

She sang the song to the end, then eased her fingertips away
from the keys.

Blaine burst into applause. "You've still got it, Eden."

"Thank you," she said, her tone softer than she'd intended. She looked away, reeling from the intimacy of the moment. Having him as a spectator to her impassioned singing felt too familiar, too reminiscent of a time she'd fought hard to forget.

"I'm not just gassing you up, either." His tone quiet, almost reverent, he took a few slow steps until he was right next to her. "I hear singing all day, every day. But I've never, ever come across another voice like yours."

She sucked in a breath, and his rich, woodsy cologne flooded her senses, threatening to undo her. Blowing the breath out, she struggled to find words to articulate her feelings. "I appreciate the compliment, Blaine. I really do. But…"

"But what?" He watched her intently. "Is something wrong?"

She tucked in her bottom lip. *How can I tell him that being this close to him ruins my concentration? That I can't focus on my work because all I want to do is climb him like a tree?*

"Eden?"

"I'm fine." She shifted on the stool, angling her face away from him in hopes that she might regain some of her faculties. His physical size, combined with his overt masculine energy, seemed to fill the space around her, making the booth feel even smaller than it actually was.

He reached out, his fingertips brushing lightly over her bare shoulder. "Are you sure?"

She trembled, reacting to the tingling sensation brought on by his electric touch. For a moment, she wanted him to continue, wanted to feel his kiss. Soon, though, common sense took over, and she shook her head. "Yes, Blaine. I'm positive."

*Will Eden be able to maintain her resolve?*

*Don't miss what happens next in…*
After Hours Redemption *by Kianna Alexander.*

*Available October 2020 wherever*
*Harlequin Desire books and ebooks are sold.*

Harlequin.com

Copyright © 2020 by Eboni Manning

HDEXP0920

# Get 4 FREE REWARDS!

## We'll send you 2 FREE Books <u>plus</u> 2 FREE Mystery Gifts.

Harlequin Desire® books transport you to the world of the American elite with juicy plot twists, delicious sensuality and intriguing scandal.

**FREE**
Value Over
**$20**

**YES!** Please send me 2 FREE Harlequin Desire novels and my 2 FREE gifts (gifts are worth about $10 retail). After receiving them, if I don't wish to receive any more books, I can return the shipping statement marked "cancel." If I don't cancel, I will receive 6 brand-new novels every month and be billed just $4.55 per book in the U.S. or $5.24 per book in Canada. That's a savings of at least 13% off the cover price! It's quite a bargain! Shipping and handling is just 50¢ per book in the U.S. and $1.25 per book in Canada.* I understand that accepting the 2 free books and gifts places me under no obligation to buy anything. I can always return a shipment and cancel at any time. The free books and gifts are mine to keep no matter what I decide.

225/326 HDN GNND

Name (please print)

Address                                                                                          Apt. #

City                                    State/Province                          Zip/Postal Code

Email: Please check this box ☐ if you would like to receive newsletters and promotional emails from Harlequin Enterprises ULC and its affiliates. You can unsubscribe anytime.

### Mail to the **Reader Service:**
**IN U.S.A.:** P.O. Box 1341, Buffalo, NY 14240-8531
**IN CANADA:** P.O. Box 603, Fort Erie, Ontario L2A 5X3

Want to try 2 free books from another series? Call 1-800-873-8635 or visit www.ReaderService.com.

*Terms and prices subject to change without notice. Prices do not include sales taxes, which will be charged (if applicable) based on your state or country of residence. Canadian residents will be charged applicable taxes. Offer not valid in Quebec. This offer is limited to one order per household. Books received may not be as shown. Not valid for current subscribers to Harlequin Desire books. All orders subject to approval. Credit or debit balances in a customer's account(s) may be offset by any other outstanding balance owed by or to the customer. Please allow 4 to 6 weeks for delivery. Offer available while quantities last.

**Your Privacy**—Your information is being collected by Harlequin Enterprises ULC, operating as Reader Service. For a complete summary of the information we collect, how we use this information and to whom it is disclosed, please visit our privacy notice located at corporate.harlequin.com/privacy-notice. From time to time we may also exchange your personal information with reputable third parties. If you wish to opt out of this sharing of your personal information, please visit readerservice.com/consumerschoice or call 1-800-873-8635. **Notice to California Residents**—Under California law, you have specific rights to control and access your data. For more information on these rights and how to exercise them, visit corporate.harlequin.com/california-privacy.

HD20R2

From acclaimed author

# ADRIANA HERRERA

*Starting over is more about who you're with than where you live…*

Running the charitable foundation of one of the most iconic high fashion department stores in the world is serious #lifegoals for ex–New Yorker Julia del Mar Ortiz, so she's determined to stick it out in Dallas—despite the efforts of the blue-eyed, smart-mouthed consultant who intends to put her job on the chopping block.

When Julia is tasked with making sure Rocco sees how valuable the programs she runs are, she's caught between a rock and a very hard set of abs. Because Rocco Quinn is almost impossible to hate—and even harder to resist.

"Herrera excels at creating the kind of rich emotional connections between her protagonists that romance readers will find irresistible." —*Booklist* on *American Dreamer*

### Order your copy now!

**carina press**

CarinaPress.com

CARAHHTS0920

## SPECIAL EXCERPT FROM

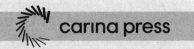

*At Dallas's iconic luxury department store, you can feel good about indulging a little...or a lot. The staff is proud of their store. If you're one of them, you're three things: brilliant, boss and bomb.*

*Julia del Mar Ortiz moved to Texas with her boyfriend, who ended up ditching her and running back to New York after only a few weeks. Left with a massive— by NYC standards, anyway—apartment and the job opportunity of a lifetime, Julia is struggling... except that's not completely true...*

*Read on for a sneak preview of*
**Here to Stay**
*by Adriana Herrera,*
*available now from Carina Press.*

He brought his cat to dinner.

I opened the door to my apartment and found Rocco holding the little carrier we'd bought for Pulga at the pet store in one hand and in the other he had a reusable shopping bag with what looked like his contribution for dinner.

"Hey, I know you said she was uninvited." His eyebrows dipped, obviously worried I'd be pissed at this plus-one situation. I wanted to kiss him so bad, I was dizzy. "But whenever I tried to leave the house, she started mewling really loud. I think she's still dehydrated."

Boy, was I in over my head.

I smiled and tried not to let him see how his words had actually turned me into a puddle of goo. "It's fine, since she's convalescent

CAREXPAHHTS0920

and all, but once she's back in shape, she's banned from this apartment."

He gave a terse nod, still looking embarrassed. "Promise."

I waved him on, but before I could get another word in, my mom came out of my room in full "Dia de Fiesta" hair and makeup. Holidays that involved a meal meant my mother had to look like she was going to a red carpet somewhere. She was wearing an orange sheath dress with her long brown hair cascading over her shoulders and three-inch heels on her feet.

To have dinner in my cramped two-bedroom apartment.

"Rocco, you're here. *Qué bueno.*" She leaned over and kissed him on the cheek, then gestured toward the living room. "Julita, I'm so glad you invited him. We have too much food."

"Thank you for letting me join you." Rocco gave me the look that I'd been getting from my friends my entire life, that said, *Damn, your mom is hot.* It was not easy to shine whenever my mother was around, but we were still obligated to try.

I'd complied with a dark green wrap dress and a little bit of mascara and lip stain, but I was nowhere near as made-up as she was. Except now I wished I'd made more of an effort, and why was I comparing myself to my mom and why did I care what Rocco thought?

I was about to say something, anything, to get myself out of this mindfucky headspace when he walked into my living room and, as he'd done with my mom, bent his head and brushed a kiss against my cheek. As he pulled back, he looked at me appreciatively, his gaze caressing me from head to toe.

"You look beautiful." There was fluttering occurring inside me again, and for a second I really wished I could just push up and kiss him. Or punch him. God, I was a mess.

*Don't miss what happens next...*
Here to Stay *by Adriana Herrera*
*available wherever Carina Press books*
*and ebooks are sold.*

CarinaPress.com

Copyright © 2020 by Adriana Herrera

CAREXPAHHTS0920